TIED TO MURDER

By

John C. Dalglish

2014

Prologue

After slipping through the crack in the door, he slowly closed it behind him. Making sure it didn't click, he turned and listened. The sun hadn't peaked over the horizon yet, but caution was required. If his target were already awake, it would make what he had to do much more difficult.

Moving carefully across the small living room, his ears picked up the sound of snoring. He looked into the bedroom and saw his target lying on her back, asleep. As he waited for the right moment, he mentally rehearsed every move he was about to make.

Once he decided to go, he rushed across the room, jumped on the bed, and covered the woman's mouth with his hand.

Her eyes flew open, confused at first, but her expression quickly changed to terror as what was happening dawned on her. He drew a knife and showed it to her. Her eyes grew wider still and she froze. He drove the knife into the pillow next to her head and moved his finger to his lips, warning her to be quiet. She nodded.

Reaching into his jacket pocket, he pulled out a roll of duct tape. Using his teeth, he tore a strip loose and forced it over her mouth. Now that both hands were free, he took out a piece of rope, flipped her on her side, pulled both of the woman's arms behind her, grabbed one leg, and tied her up in seconds. He got up off the bed.

Walking into the kitchen, he looked under the sink, in the closet, and in the drawers. Finally, he found what he was after. Tearing one loose, he walked back to the bedroom, and sat beside the tiny woman. Snapping the garbage bag in the air until it opened, he dragged it over her head as she struggled to get free.

Grabbing the role of duct tape, he wrapped a long piece around her neck, sealing the bag over her.

He got up and walked to the bedroom door. Leaning against the doorframe, he watched until she stopped kicking and her body lay still.

Before leaving, he walked over to the bed, grabbed the loose end of the rope, and released it. Taking the rope, the knife, and the tape, he left the room. Going to the air conditioning control, he turned it down as low as it could go. The sun was just starting to come up when he unlocked the patio door and slipped away.

Chapter 1

"Come On, Ruby! We're going to be late."

Grace Caldwell hated being late, and her sister Ruby was perpetually running behind schedule. Grace stood by the door of their apartment and stared at the hallway mirror.

At seventy-four, she was only three years older than her sister, but somehow Ruby managed to look ten years her junior. Grace attributed looking older to constantly worrying about her baby sister. Even now, she felt like she had to watch out for Ruby.

She turned sideways and looked at her profile. Five-foot even, short gray hair and blue eyes, she was happy with the way she'd aged. The men in the complex still showed an interest in her.

"I'm coming, I'm coming. Don't get your girdle in a wad."

Ruby was four inches taller than Grace, with their father's red hair. With bright green eyes, Ruby could still turn the head of a younger man.

Grace was sure Ruby had also inherited their father's temper. "We've played cards every Wednesday night for the last five years. You'd think you might be on time just once."

Ruby just smiled at her. Grace knew it didn't bother Ruby at all to fluster her big sister occasionally.

"Maybe next week."

Grace rolled her eyes and opened the door to the apartment.

They shared a two-bedroom unit in Orchid Village, a retirement community consisting of multiple unit buildings, all on cul-de-sacs named after orchids.

A large community center was the hub in a giant wheel, the individual buildings at the end of roads running away from the center like spokes in a wheel. Grace had rented the unit almost ten years ago after her husband had passed away.

Four years later, Ruby called with the news her scumbag husband had left. It came as neither a surprise nor a disappointment to Grace. She told her sister to sell everything and come live with her. They'd been roommates ever since.

Grace drove up to the clubhouse fifteen minutes late. The building was divided into offices and colored rooms, each color having a different use. Red for reading, green for exercise, blue for cards, and so on. Going inside, they found two members of their group already waiting at a card table in the Blue Room.

As the women approached their friends, Grace bent over to kiss Tabby on the cheek. "Sorry we're late."

Tonya 'Tabby' Jensen was the self-appointed worrier of the group. If someone was missing, ill, or out of sugar, it was Tabby who made sure the problem got solved.

The youngest woman of the group at sixty-eight, she kept her brown hair, with very little gray, cut shoulder length. Willie thought it had to be dyed, but Tabby wouldn't admit to it. She wore jogging suits and tennis shoes because she thought they made her look younger.

"Don't worry about it. Ruth isn't here yet, either."

Grace watched as Ruby wrapped her arms around Willie.

"Hi, Wild Bill! Miss me?"

He smiled wide and hugged her back. "Of course!"

Willie, or 'Wild Bill' as Ruby liked to call him, was a sixty-six-year-old widower with a booming laugh and immense gleaming smile that contrasted with his dark skin. Grace had watched Willie's easygoing nature help settle Ruby in when she first arrived. They'd been buddies ever since.

Grace took a seat and pulled out her cell phone. Punching Ruth's number, she let it ring at least ten times before hanging up. She looked at Tabby.

"No answer."

Ruby piped up. "She's probably got a male visitor."

Tabby made a face, and Grace couldn't tell if it was one of disgust or worry.

"Maybe she's on her way. Anybody talk to her today?"

Heads shook all around the table. Grace refused to worry yet.

"Well, let's play some gin and see if she turns up."

****

An hour later, Ruth had neither showed up nor called. Numerous calls to her phone had gone unanswered, and worrywart Tabby was nearing full-blown panic.

"We need to check on her."

Grace agreed. Ruth never missed their card games.

"Do you still have the spare key she gave you?"

Tabby nodded.

"Okay, who wants to go?"

Willie got up. "I'll go. I need to use the bathroom anyway."

Tabby fished the chain with everyone's spare keys out of her purse. She kept the group's keys as a safety measure, mostly for her own peace of mind. She tossed it to Willie. "The names are on the tags."

Willie caught the keys easily, and left to check on their friend.

****

Ruth Rogers lived on the branch of Orchid Village known as Fox Tail Court. Willie stopped his '85 Chevy pickup at the entrance to the building. At her door, he rang the bell.

When no answer came, he banged on the door with his fist.

"Ruth!"

Still without a response, he took out the key and let himself in.

"Ruth?"

As he moved through her apartment, he realized how cold it was.

"Ruth? Dang it, why's it so cold in here?"

He got to the bedroom door and stopped. As his brain struggled to process the scene, he moved toward the bed. When he touched her tiny cold foot, his hand instinctively jerked away.

Staggering backward, his eyes fixed on the garbage bag over his friend's head, he pulled his cell phone from his pocket. Despite trembling fingers, he managed to dial 9-1-1.

****

Grace looked up from her cards to the clock on the wall. Willie had been gone nearly forty minutes. Suddenly, the interior of the game room lit up with flashing red and blue lights.

Tabby looked up at the same time as Ruby, and they echoed each other. "What's going on?"

Grace laid her cards down and went to the window.

"Police cars."

After watching the last of several cars go by, she turned to the other two women.

"They're going toward Ruth's building!"

Chapter 2

Detective Jason Strong came running through the front doors of the San Antonio police station. For the third day in a row, he was late. His partner, Vanessa Layne, rolled her big, blue eyes and made an exaggerated display of checking her watch.

Jason knew she was just taking the opportunity to needle him, but he still didn't like to be late.

"Sorry, partner."

"Same thing as the last two days?"

"Yeah. Poor thing is really having a tough time of it."

He sat down at his desk, which butted up against his partner's, so they faced each other. The 'poor thing' he was referring to was his wife, Sandy. Pregnant for the first time, her morning sickness was bad.

Vanessa could sympathize. Her son, Kasen, now almost a year old, had caused her the same problem early on.

"Morning sickness is no fun."

"Why do they call it morning sickness, anyway? She seems to have waves of nausea at all hours of the day."

Vanessa laughed. "Most women get sick in the morning, but there's no law, that's for sure."

Jason looked around the station. Homicide, which occupied the entire third floor of the station, was usually buzzing with activity. This morning was quiet, and even the lieutenant's office was empty.

"Where's the lieutenant?"

"He went downstairs to talk with Doc Josie."

Jason nodded. Doctor Jocelyn Carter, 'Doc Josie' to everyone at the station, was the head of the Forensic Science Department.

The phone in the lieutenant's office started to ring. Vanessa got up and answered it.

"Lieutenant Patton's office."

Jason watched her as she grabbed a piece of paper and took down some information. She looked in his direction as she hung up.

"Patrol called. They've got a body at Orchid Village."

"The retirement community? Why us?"

"It's clearly *not* death by natural causes. You want to get your car while I notify the lieutenant?"

"Sounds good."

They got on the elevator, pushing *One* for Jason, and *Basement* for Vanessa. The elevator stopped and Jason stepped out.

"Meet you outside in ten?"

"Okay."

The elevator doors closed and Jason turned to go to the parking lot.

"Hey, Jason."

Jason looked up to see his friend Dave Connor. Dave had lost his wife a few months ago, and he'd been on leave. Her death had been a big case for Jason and Vanessa. They'd almost lost the lieutenant to the same killer.

Jason had stayed in contact with Dave and finally convinced him to come back to work. Dave manned the Sergeant's desk, directing lobby traffic. An old injury had put him behind the desk, which he hated, but Jason knew being back at the station was the best medicine for his friend.

"Dave! How ya doin'?"

"Makin' it. You?"

"Sandy's still struggling with morning sickness. Me, I'm doing fine."

Dave laughed. "Yeah, us guys sure got the better end of the deal when it comes to pregnancy."

Jason chuckled. "Amen to that! See ya later."

Jason stepped out of the station doors into the heat of the early South Texas summer. Spring was barely over, but they'd already had four one-hundred-plus-degree days. Not a good sign for this moisture-starved area of the Lone Star State.

Getting in his car, he cranked the air conditioning and pulled up by the station doors. Vanessa climbed into the passenger seat a few minutes later.

"The lieutenant called Doc Davis. He's got a van headed to the scene."

Doctor Leonard Davis, one of the smartest people Jason had ever met, had been City Coroner for as long as Jason could remember.

"What about forensics?"

"Also on the way."

"Okay. Let's go see what we've got."

****

Fifteen minutes later, they pulled up at the front gate of Orchid Village. Located on

15

the north end of the city, the retirement community was well known for its immense size and active retiree population.

Jason pulled onto the main road, known as Orchid Way, and spotted flashing lights among a group of buildings to his right. He followed the road around and pulled up at the edge of the crowd. Vanessa got out and cleared a path for Jason to drive up to the crime tape.

An officer lifted the tape for the car to pass through. As Jason got out, Vanessa caught up to him. She looked back over her shoulder at the crowd.

"I've seen big crowds at crime scenes but this takes the cake. There must be a thousand people here."

Jason gave her a grim smile.

"Must be all the flashing lights brought on by a dead body!"

Vanessa snorted. "Must be."

They walked up the path leading to the ground floor apartment. The forensic team was already there, but they were waiting for the detectives to get their first look before moving anything.

The two detectives went through the front door and back to the bedroom. Jason wasn't prepared for the scene that greeted them.

"Is that a garbage bag over her head?"

"Yes," The voice was female, but it didn't belong to Vanessa. Jason turned to see a young officer looking at him. "We found a box of matching bags on the counter in the kitchen."

Vanessa was leaning over the body.

"What's around her neck?"

"Duct tape."

"Jason, look at this pillow. Knife?"

He walked over and peered closely.

"I'd say so." He turned to the female officer. "Any knives found?"

The officer shook her head.

"Kitchen knives are in a drawer. Hard to tell if one is missing."

Jason rubbed his arms.

"Why's it so cold in here?"

The officer pointed toward the living room.

"A/C was left on at its lowest setting. We assume by the killer."

"Seems pretty comfortable to me." Jason turned to see Doc Davis coming through the door.

"Of course! You like it because it reminds you of home, your morgue!"

Doc Davis smiled and shook Jason's hand. He waved at Vanessa.

"Hi, Vanessa."

"Hi, Doc. I'm impressed with the personal appearance. No underling this time?"

"I heard you were going to be here, so I came myself."

"Flattery will get you everywhere, Doc."

He smiled and then, as he approached the body, slid a pair of gloves on. Carefully, he pushed a finger under the tape around the woman's neck.

"The tape's not tight enough to have choked the victim. Probably just meant to hold the bag in place."

Jason walked over and looked more closely at the victim.

"Any sign of restraints?"

"By the position of the body, I would say probably. She's lying with both hands behind her."

Doc Davis gently lifted each hand.

"Something restrained her. She's got ligature marks on both wrists."

"Any guess of what was used?"

"Looks to be rope, but can't say for sure until the autopsy."

Vanessa was talking to the female officer, writing some information on her pad, and turned to Jason.

"The guy who found her is sitting on the patio. You want to go talk to him with me?"

Chapter 3

Jason and Vanessa found the man who called 9-1-1, but as they stepped out onto the patio, Jason hesitated.

"I'll be out in a minute."

He returned to the female officer.

"You were the first to respond?"

"Yes, sir."

"Was the patio door locked?"

She didn't answer immediately, and Jason could tell she wasn't sure.

"It's okay, Officer. Just tell me what you remember."

"I'm sorry, Detective. I just don't know. I didn't check it before Mr. Davis went out to the patio."

Jason knew he should chew her out so it wouldn't happen again, but he'd been a young cop once, and he knew how it felt.

He looked her in the eyes and lowered his voice. "Always check and secure the perimeter of any scene. Learn, and make sure next time, understand?"

He could see gratitude in her eyes.

"Yes, sir. Thank you."

He turned and went back to the patio.

Vanessa was sitting across the table from an elderly man, who looked drawn and tired. She was asking questions and making notes. Jason interrupted.

"Excuse me. My name is Detective Strong..."

Jason waited until the man turned his direction. Vanessa introduced the man.

"This is Willie Davis. He found our victim, Ruth Rogers."

"Hello, Mr. Davis. Do you remember if this door was locked when you came outside?"

Willie scrunched his face, trying to remember, but finally shook his head.

"I don't think so, but I'm not sure. I'm sorry."

Jason touched the man's shoulder.

"It's okay. Do you remember if the *front* door was locked?"

"Yes. I used the spare key to let myself in."

"Thank you."

Jason turned back to the sliding door and examined the handle. He couldn't find any sign of forced entry. He went back into the apartment and checked the front door. It looked undamaged, as well. He returned to the patio.

Vanessa was finishing with Mr. Davis. "Why did you decide to check on Mrs. Rogers?"

"Ruth never missed our weekly card game and we hadn't heard from her. I came to make sure she was okay... That's when I found her."

Vanessa and Jason exchanged glances. Jason sat down next to Willie.

"This card game, is it regular?"

"Every Wednesday."

"The same group?"

"Yes. Me, Ruth, Fred Murphy, Tonya Jensen, Ruby Pryor, and her sister, Grace Caldwell."

"Was everyone else at the card game?"

"Everyone except Fred. He's visiting his granddaughter in Florida."

Vanessa had been writing names and notes as fast as she could. She looked up.

"Have you called your friends?"

"Not yet."

"Can you call them now?"

"I guess. I don't know how I'm going to tell them about Ruth, though."

Jason felt for the man. Delivering news like a friend's death was very difficult under the best of circumstances, but a sudden death like murder was the worst.

"I'd like to ask a few questions of each of them. Can you call them and ask all of them to come up to the crime tape? I'll meet them there, and I'll tell them."

"Thanks, Detective, but it'd probably be easier coming from me."

"Okay. Tell them to ask for Detective Strong, and I'll bring them here."

Willie pulled out his cell phone and pushed a number. After a few moments, someone answered.

"Tabby, it's Willie."

Jason and Vanessa watched as he moved his head up and down.

"I know, Tabby. I'm with the police now."

More waiting, and Jason could tell the person on the other end was very agitated.

"Tabby…Tabby, listen to me. Are the others with you?"

This time Jason could hear her positive reply. Willie plowed on before she could get started rambling again.

"Okay, bring everybody to the end of Fox Tail. Tell the officer at the police tape to call Detective Strong."

The pain on Willie's face ate a Jason. How did you tell a close-knit group one of their own was gone?

"Yes, Tabby. Detective Strong, and bring everybody."

He hung up and looked at the detectives.

"They're still at the clubhouse. She said less than five minutes."

Jason excused himself and went to meet the rest of the group.

Chapter 4

Vanessa watched Jason leave before turning to Willie.

"Will you be alright for a few minutes?"

"Yes, I'm okay."

"Good. I'll be back shortly."

Vanessa got up and went back into the apartment. She found Doc Davis packing up his case to leave. Bright flashes from the forensic tech's camera bounced off the walls.

"What's the early word, Doc?"

Doc Davis snapped his case shut.

He looked at least sixty-five, with just a ring of gray hair around his head, and extremely pale skin from too many days in the basement morgue. Nonetheless, retirement was a dirty word around the Chief Medical Examiner. He weighed on the heavy side of two-hundred-fifty pounds, and his knees groaned as he stood.

"Suffocation, likely. No sign of strangulation, so she was probably tied first, then the bag was put over her head."

Vanessa shivered inside at the thought of the poor woman struggling for her last breaths.

"Any sign of rape?"

"Not that I can see here. Underwear still on, no obvious bruising around the genital area, but I can't say for sure until autopsy."

"What about time of death?"

"The air conditioning was probably so cold to try and throw us off, but I'd be surprised if T.O.D. was more than forty-eight hours ago, probably less."

"Thanks, Doc. I'll fill Jason in."

Doc Davis nodded and Vanessa went back outside to find Jason. He was standing on the lawn, watching Willie tell his friends the news. Vanessa walked over to him. "How's he doing?"

"Okay, I guess. I don't think Willie is a stranger to death. My guess is he has a military background."

"I spoke with Doc Davis. He thinks she was tied first, and then the bag put on her head. Suffocation, not strangulation. No sign of rape, and he puts the T.O.D. at less than forty-eight hours."

Jason nodded.

Willie turned and waved at the two detectives. They went over and Jason took a seat, while Vanessa stayed standing. She took out her notepad.

Jason started with the woman who introduced herself as Tabby.

"I'm very sorry for your loss. I know answering questions right after news like this is hard, but we need whatever information you can give us."

She nodded stiffly. "I understand."

"Your full name is?"

"Tonya Barbara Jensen. I live in Building A, on Dancing Doll Drive."

"When was the last time you saw Ruth?"

"I haven't seen her since our last card game, but I talked to her Monday morning. She seemed fine."

Jason asked each member of the group about the last time they saw or spoke to Ruth Rogers. Finally, he directed his last question to all of them.

"Does anyone have any suggestion who might want to hurt your friend?"

They shook their heads in unison.

Jason stood up and Vanessa nodded at him. They were done.

The two detectives left the friends to mourn their loss, going back into the apartment to have a final look around. Someone had finally turned the air conditioning off, and it was now slightly above meat locker temperature inside.

Jason made sure the tape, the garbage bag, and the box it came from, were all safely bagged and tagged for evidence before they left. Vanessa followed him to the door.

"Back to the station?"

Jason shook his head.

"Seems like all this commotion would have the manager of the complex nearby. Let's find him."

****

They found the manager in his office at the community building. A tall, thin man with sandy hair, and a good tan, 'Surfer dude' was the first thing to pop into Jason's head.

He wore a purple Orchid Village shirt with the name 'Steve Jaffe' embroidered over the pocket. He looked up from his desk as the detectives entered.

"Can I help you?"

Jason displayed his badge.

"I'm Detective Strong, and this is my partner, Detective Layne. We'd like to ask you a few questions."

Steve stood up, shook Jason's hand, and gave a nod to Vanessa standing by the door.

"This must be connected to all the emergency lights over on Fox Tail Court."

"It is. I'm afraid there's been a murder in your complex."

Steve sat back down, and to Jason, his shock looked genuine.

"Murder?"

"Yes."

"I thought it was just a medical emergency for one of our residents. Who was killed?"

"Her name is Ruth Rogers. Do you know her?"

"Sure, she's one of our long-time tenants. What happened?"

"I'm sorry, but I can't discuss details of the case. Can you tell me if Ruth Rogers had any enemies in the complex? Maybe someone she was having a dispute with?"

Steve shook his head.

"No, nobody comes to mind. In fact, I've never had any problem with her."

"Okay. I would like to speak with all of your employees, and anyone else, who is regularly working in and around the buildings."

"I'll need to talk to the owner, but I don't imagine it will be a problem."

Vanessa opened her notepad.

"Who's the owner?"

"Marcus Winston."

Vanessa looked up from her pad.

"One man? I thought a complex this huge would be owned by a corporation."

"Well, technically it is, but in name only. Marcus Winston built Orchid Village and still runs it."

"How do we reach Mr. Winston?"

"He's out of town. A new Orchid Village is being built in Austin," Steve reached for a card on the desk. "This is his card."

Jason took it and gave one of his own to the manager.

"What about security? Do you have your own security team?"

"Well, team might be a strong word for it. We have two employees who work the overnight. They watch the gates, and occasionally, they'll take a spin around the complex in a golf cart. They're here to watch the office and community buildings more than anything else."

"Who was on guard last night?"

Steve took out his phone, pushed a couple buttons until he found what he was looking for. "His name is Tom Baxter. His number is 555-3424."

Vanessa wrote it down and the detectives turned to leave. Steve Jaffe stopped them.

"Does this have any connection to the missing man from Building C on Striped Tiger Way?"

Jason turned back.

"Someone went missing? When?"

"Last month. One of your detectives was handling the case."

The manager went to a corkboard on the wall and removed a card.

"Detective Jefferson."

"Nina Jefferson?"

The manager nodded. Jason and Vanessa exchanged surprised looks.

Jason shook his head. "I don't know if there's a connection, but I'll talk to Detective Jefferson. Can you fax that employee list to the number on my card?"

"Sure."

Once outside, Jason pulled out his phone and called the station. Nina Jefferson was off duty and Jason decided that since it wasn't that urgent, he'd try and reach her in the morning.

Next, he dialed the number Vanessa had written down for the security guard. He got an answering machine, and left a message for Tom Baxter to call him.

He looked at Vanessa. "Back to the Bat Cave?"

She grinned.

"You can be so hokey sometimes."

Chapter 5

The next morning, Jason was on time for a change, but stopped on the second floor to see Detective Nina Jefferson. He found her at her desk in Missing Persons.

Detective Nina Jefferson is short and stocky, with rich, dark skin, brown eyes, and curly black hair. Jason and Vanessa had met her when they were investigating a serial killer case. At that time, she was a detective with Austin PD, and they liked her immediately.

Last year, she had accepted a position with SAPD in Missing Persons, under Lieutenant Sarah Banks, and moved to San Antonio. Her face lit up when she saw Jason coming.

"Jason! How's things in the Bat Cave?"

He smiled. "I take it you've already talked to Vanessa."

She let a sly grin crease her face.

"First thing this morning. She made some copies of my file on the missing guy from Orchid Village."

"Great. I'll let her fill me in." He looked around the office. "How's life with Lieutenant Banks?"

"Good. She's demanding, you already know that, but she has your back. I like her."

"Glad to hear it. I guess I'd better go catch up with Vanessa. Take care."

Jason hopped back on the elevator and rode to the third floor. He found Vanessa by the coffee machine.

"Good morning."

She offered him a cup. "Late again. Sandy still having trouble?"

"No. She's a little better today. I was actually on time today, but stopped to talk to Nina Jefferson."

"Beat ya to it."

"So I gathered. Learn anything?"

He followed Vanessa back to her desk, where she picked up a file and handed it to him.

"Darrel Patterson, seventy-nine, went missing three weeks ago. There's still no sign of him. He disappeared during the night." She sat down. "People saw him enter his apartment the night before, but he didn't show for an appointment the next day."

Jason flipped through the file. "Any forensic information?"

"Nope. No sign of forced entry, and the doors were locked when police showed up to do a wellness check."

Jason sat down at his own desk.

"Any prints?"

"None, at least none that were unaccounted for."

"Any sign of a struggle?"

"No. Nina believes he either went with someone he knew or was coerced by a weapon."

Jason closed the file.

"So nothing to help our case?"

"Afraid not."

Their lieutenant came up while they were talking and handed Jason three sheets of paper.

"These just came in on the fax."

Lieutenant John Patton was a big man. He worked out regularly and was in tremendous shape. Balding, he liked to claim his hair had moved to his eyebrows and moustache, both of which were unruly.

Patton had hired Jason and was more than just his lieutenant; he was a friend.

"How's things coming on the Orchid Village case?"

"Not much to go on right now. This list of employees gives us a place to start.

We'll go interview these folks. Maybe someone saw something."

"Good. Keep me up to date. Those of us here in the Bat Cave don't like being left in the dark."

Vanessa laughed aloud, then caught herself. Jason glared at her.

"Yes, sir."

When the lieutenant walked away, Jason stared at Vanessa.

"You're having fun with this, aren't you?"

"Yeah, I kinda like being Batgirl."

Jason laughed, both at her and at himself.

"Come on, Nut-girl. We've got interviews to do."

****

While Jason drove to Orchid Village, Vanessa went over the list of Orchid Village employees that had been faxed over.

"Maintenance chief is Gary Doan, thirty-seven, been with Orchid for five years. He has two men who work under him. Both men with the company less than a year."

She flipped the page.

"Head gardener is Jose Jimenez, forty-two, been with Orchid for eight years. He

John C. Dalglish

has three men and two women on his crew, and they appear to have been with Orchid almost as long as their boss."

Jason turned into Orchid Village and parked at the community building.

"I called ahead and the manager said the landscape crew always eats lunch together about this time each day. He said we could talk to all of them at once."

They got out of the car and went inside the main building. They found Steve Jaffe sitting in his office.

"Hello, detectives. The landscaping crew is in the lunchroom. It's this way."

The manager led them through a set of double doors into a brightly lit room. Tables lined one side of the room with vending machines glowing along the opposite wall. A sink and microwave were at the far end.

Steve introduced them before excusing himself.

"Detectives, this is Jose Jimenez and his crew. They'll be happy to answer any questions you have."

Jose didn't get up. In fact, nobody moved. Jason took a seat at the table while Vanessa stayed standing, her notepad out. Jason started with the head gardener.

"We want to thank you for taking time out to talk to us during your lunch."

Jimenez didn't look up.

"Didn't seem we had much choice."

Jason and Vanessa exchanged silent looks of surprise.

"Did you hear about the events of last night?"

"If you mean Ruth Rogers dying, we heard."

"We were hoping one of you may have seen or heard something." Jason looked from one crewmember to the next. "Did you notice anything unusual in the last few days?"

"Nope," Jimenez answered, while nobody else said anything. In fact, Jason noticed they kept their eyes averted from his.

"How about your crew, did any of you see anything unusual?"

"They didn't see nothin.'" Jimenez again.

Jason was getting impatient.

"I'd like them to answer for themselves."

Jose Jimenez stood up, staring down at the detective.

"Look, we know how this works. Some white lady gets killed, and the first ones you suspect are the Mexican gardeners. Well, we didn't see nothin,' and we don't know nothin.' We answered your questions. Now can we finish our lunch in peace?"

Jason stood, matching the man's stare.

"Nobody is accusing you, or your crew, of anything. We're just looking for help finding a killer. I don't know where you get the idea you're a suspect because you're Mexican, but if you can help me catch a murderer, I don't care if you're an Eskimo or an elephant. Are we clear?"

Jimenez sat back down.

"Yeah, we're clear."

Jason took out a card and threw it on the table.

"If you think of anything, call us."

Jimenez grabbed the card and tossed it at the trashcan in the corner. It fluttered to the floor.

Jason walked over and picked up the card. Vanessa put her pad away as her partner walked back to the table. He set the card down, out of the reach of the chief gardener, and repeated his previous statement.

"If any of you think of something, call us." He stared at Jose, daring him to pick up the card again. This time the gardener ignored it, and the two detectives left.

****

Next up was the maintenance crew. Steve Jaffe told them where the crew was working, and the two detectives decided it was close enough to walk. Vanessa said it for both of them

"Mr. Jimenez certainly has issues."

"I'll say. Probably got a couple illegals on his crew. He may just be protecting them."

"Yeah, or he's hiding something darker."

"That's a distinct possibility."

Jason looked around them as they walked.

"This place is huge. It's not until you walk around that you really feel how immense it is."

"Yeah. It's pretty impressive."

They arrived at Building B on Lady Slipper Drive. Gary Doan and his crew were working on the second floor. Vanessa took the lead this time.

"Gary Doan?"

"Yeah, that's me. You must be the detectives Steve told me about."

"Yes. I'm Detective Layne, and this is my partner, Detective Strong."

Gary Doan stepped over a toolbox and shook hands with both detectives.

"Nice to meet you. Terrible business, what happened to Ruth."

"You knew the victim?"

"Sure, been here a long time. Nice lady."

"Did you notice anything or anyone unusual the last few days?"

"No. Not me, but I stay pretty busy."

"Can we ask your crew?"

"By all means."

Vanessa posed the same question to each member of the team and received a similar answer. They weren't getting anywhere.

They thanked Gary and his crew for their time and started back for the car. Jason looked at his notes.

"Pretty much a blank page. You do any better?"

"Just a note to look into Jose Jimenez's record."

"Seems like a good idea. Let's go back to the station and see what Doc Davis has for us. He was supposed to do the autopsy this morning."

Jason's phone rang.

"Detective Strong."

"Yeah, this is Tom Baxter. I had a message to call you."

"Yes, Tom. You were on duty at Orchid Valley last night?"

"Yes, sir."

"Did you hear what happened?"

"I saw it on the news, but I didn't have anything out of the ordinary occur on my shift. I made my regular rounds and all was quiet. It's pretty sleepy there after about nine o'clock."

"I imagine it is. What about vehicles coming and going through the gate? Anyone unusual?"

"Not that I remember. There's a lot of cars in that complex. I probably wouldn't know one didn't belong unless it was very unusual."

"I understand. Thank you for calling, and if you think of anything, please call back."

"Yes sir, I sure will."

Jason hung up and continued walking back to the office with Vanessa. Jason shook his head.

"That was the security guard. He said nothing was out the ordinary last night." Jason chuckled. "He probably has a hard time just staying awake most nights."

Vanessa laughed. "I know I would!"

When they got back to the car, Jason went inside to say goodbye to Steve Jaffe.

"We're done, Steve. Thanks for your help."

"No problem. Anything else, you let me know."

"Actually, do you have a map of Orchid Village?"

"Sure."

"Can I get a copy?"

"Of course."

The manager pulled open a filing cabinet drawer and retrieved a piece of paper, handing it to Jason.

"Anything else?"

"Just one thing; do you know when Mr. Winston will be back in town?"

"I expect him back tomorrow morning. That was the last I heard."

"Okay. Have him call me, will you?"

"Of course."

Jason said goodbye and went out to the car. He handed the map to Vanessa.

"I thought we might do some plotting on this map."

Vanessa looked at it.

"Seems like a good idea."

Chapter 6

Jason and Vanessa arrived back at the station after stopping for a quick bite. Instead of going upstairs to the third floor, Vanessa pushed the elevator button for the basement.

When the doors slid open, they stepped out.

To the left was the domain of the Medical Examiner, Doc Davis. His office consisted of an autopsy room, two large freezers for bodies, and a small, glass-walled cubicle where he did his paperwork.

Straight ahead, down a long hallway, was Records. If they turned right, they'd find themselves in the Forensic Science Department, run by Doctor Jocelyn Carter.

They turned left and pushed through the white doors. Doc Davis was standing with his back to them, speaking into a microphone hung from the ceiling above the autopsy table. A body lay on the table.

Jason and Vanessa stopped and allowed him to finish his thought before making their presence known. Jason nudged Vanessa and gave her a wink.

He cleared his throat. "Is there a men's bathroom in here?"

Without turning around, the Medical Examiner answered with a huff.

"No, there's no bathroom in here. Please go back out the way you came in."

Jason persisted.

"A detective told me it was in here."

"The detective was wrong. It happens more than you might think."

Vanessa picked up the prank.

"Is there a woman's bathroom in here?"

Doc Davis spun from his table.

"No! There's no…" He caught sight of the two detectives grinning at him. "Oh, it's you two. I should have known."

Jason burst out laughing, but Vanessa played innocent.

"Does that really happen a lot, Doc?"

"You know it does. It makes me nuts, but they won't let me put a lock on the door."

He washed his hands and came over to his tormenters.

"Good to see you two. I guess you're interested in what I discovered on Mrs. Rogers?"

"Indeed. Anything we can use?"

They followed Doc Davis into his office.

"Not much." He grabbed a file on his desk and gave it to Jason. "She died from suffocation, no drugs in the tox screen, and no evidence of sexual assault."

Vanessa was taking notes.

"What about time of death? Was it consistent with what we already knew?"

"Yes, despite the cold room. I'm relatively certain she died sometime between late Tuesday night and Wednesday morning."

Jason handed the file back.

"Anything else?"

"Just one thing. She had a third ligature mark on her right ankle."

"Her ankle?"

"Yeah, and all three were rope burns. It looks like she was tied like a calf at a rodeo."

"A calf?" Jason's eyebrows shot up. "Like lasso the calf, throw it down, and rope it?"

"That's what it looks like."

"Okay. Thanks, Doc."

Vanessa snapped her notepad shut and looked at Jason.

"We go across the hall next?"

Jason nodded, and jerked a thumb toward the medical examiner's office.

"Maybe Doc Josie can be more help than this fellow."

Doc Davis rolled his eyes.

"You detectives! You're always looking for someone to make your job easy."

Jason grabbed his chest.

"That hurts, Doc. By the way, is there a bathroom down here?"

The doc pointed at the door. "Out! Both of you! Now!"

Both detectives obeyed, laughing as they left.

They crossed the hallway and went through the double doors bearing the name of Doctor Jocelyn Carter, Forensic Science Department. They found her sitting at a computer.

Short with curly, brown hair and black, wire-framed glasses around blue eyes, she could have easily passed for a classic college professor. She looked up and smiled as they came in.

"Hi, guys."

Jason pulled up a chair across from where Doc Josie was sitting, while Vanessa opened her notepad.

"Hi, Doc," they said at the same time.

Doc Josie handed a file to Vanessa, who flipped through it and made some notes. Jason wanted the short version.

"What's the good word, Doc?"

"Well, let's see. The garbage bag was from the box found in the kitchen, and the tape is cheap stuff you can purchase at any home improvement or dollar store. If you find the roll, we might be able to match it."

"Any prints?"

"None. We checked the garbage bag and dusted most of the apartment. The only prints we found belonged to the victim. I do have one little tidbit for you, though."

Jason smiled.

"That's why you're the best, Doc. You never let us down."

"Usually, in a case of restraint by rope, we can find an embedded fiber or two, but nothing at all was left. Makes me think it's some sort of hard, smooth rope."

"Like a rodeo rope?"

"Maybe. Why?"

"Doc Davis said it looked like she been calf-roped," Jason got up. "Good stuff, Doc. Any hairs or DNA?"

"None."

"Okay, thanks a lot. See ya later."

They left the lab and, as they waited for the elevator, Vanessa said what was on both of their minds.

"Not much to go on."

The doors slid open and Jason pushed the button for the third floor.

"'Not much' is right."

****

As the two detectives arrived on the third floor, the lieutenant was calling their names.

"Anyone seen Strong and Layne?"

"Right here!" Jason announced.

Lieutenant Patton turned around and spotted them stepping off the elevator.

"Need you two in my office."

They followed him in and Vanessa shut the door. The lieutenant started without waiting for them to sit down.

"I just got a call from the State Park Rangers. There's a park just north of Gonzalez, and a body's been found there this afternoon. The description matches the missing guy from Orchid Village."

The lieutenant sat down and tossed a file across the desk.

"I've been in contact with Lieutenant Banks, and she released the case to us. Nina

Jefferson happens to be up in Austin. The rangers are holding the crime scene until you two can get out there." He pointed at the file. "The directions are inside. Have Doc Josie send a photographer with you, and get going."

Neither detective needed to be told a second time. They were out the door and on their way in ten minutes.

****

Palmetto State Park was just under an hour east of San Antonio on I-10. When they arrived at the front gates, the park supervisor directed them to follow the main road back to the shower house, turn right, and look for the crime tape.

It was impossible to miss. Large trees, which normally shaded campsites, were instead used as posts. The tape stretched for hundreds of feet in every direction.

Vanessa couldn't help herself.

"What do you think? These people own stock in crime scene tape?"

Jason laughed. "Maybe they just like the color."

He parked and the two detectives got out. Their cameraman was close behind.

A woman in a Park Ranger uniform came toward them. Short and round, with dirty blond hair, too much eye make-up, and a uniform two sizes too small, she struggled to walk across the uneven ground.

"Are you two the detectives from San Antonio?"

Vanessa stepped forward and extended her hand.

"Yes. I'm Detective Layne, and this is my partner, Detective Strong."

She ignored the hand.

"Great! Follow me."

They ducked under the crime tape and trailed the ranger down to the banks of the San Marcos River, which ran through the middle of the park. The ranger talked as she walked.

"Camper came down to fish this morning and found our guy. One of our rangers had seen the APB on your old man, put two and two together, and called you guys."

Vanessa looked down at the body. It was Darrell Patterson all right, and torn open over his face, was a garbage bag secured with a piece of tape.

"Was the bag open when he was found?"

The ranger nodded.

"Yup. I figured a rock or something ripped it."

Vanessa looked up and down the creek as she slipped on a pair of latex gloves.

"Where does this go?"

"It flows under I-10 to the north, and wanders for miles to the south."

"And I imagine there are an infinite number of places to access the river, where a body can be dumped in the water?"

"Yes and no. There are many places to dump a body, but most are on privately held farms. The easiest place to dump would be somewhere near the I-10 overpass."

Vanessa turned to see Jason examining the ground. "No drag marks and no tire marks. Probably floated here."

Their photographer was getting the whole scene on film. Vanessa noticed the dead man's arms were pinned under him. She bent over and rolled him onto his side.

"Jason, look at this."

Jason joined her and saw immediately what she was looking at.

"Same burns as Ruth Rogers. What about the ankles?"

Vanessa let the body roll back where it was, and examined each ankle. The right one had a burn.

Vanessa got up and walked over by the park ranger.

"Is the guy who found the body still around?"

"No. We got a statement and let him go. He was pretty shook up, but camp records indicated he showed up yesterday afternoon."

"Okay. Can we get a copy of the statement?"

"Sure. I'll get it."

As the ranger walked away, Jason came up.

"Photo guy is done. Their coroner is going to deliver the body to Doc Davis. You ready?"

"Yeah. I want to go up where I-10 crosses the river. Ranger lady says that's the most likely spot our guy went into the water."

"Sounds good. Let's go."

Chapter 7

Jason had returned to the station just long enough to drop off Vanessa and the photographer. He immediately left for the doctor's office. He and Sandy had an appointment for an ultrasound.

Jason pulled into the medical building parking lot to find Sandy just getting out of her car. She smiled and walked over to where he was parking.

Sandy was tall, almost the same height as Jason, with blonde hair and brown eyes. She was just beginning to show and the kids in her classroom had asked if she was okay. She told them her surprise, and they were almost as excited as Jason had been.

She kissed him and hooked her arm through his.

"I was afraid you weren't going to make it. Patton told me you had to go east of the city."

"So you're checking up on me, are you?"

She gave him a little squeeze.

"That's right. And don't you forget it."

He pulled the door open for her.

"Yes, ma'am."

They checked in and were about to sit down when the nurse called their name. Taking them back to the sonogram room, the nurse had Sandy get up on the bed. The technician came in, greeted them, and had Sandy expose her stomach.

The tech squirted some gel on Sandy's belly, then took the probe and placed it on her.

Swirling holographs, in black and white, appeared on the screen. The technician moved the probe back and forth, searching for whatever it was she needed to see. Finally, she looked at both of them.

"Do you want to know if it's a boy or a girl?"

"Yes."

"No."

The yes came from Jason, the no from Sandy.

"Okay, no."

"All right, yes."

This time Jason said no and Sandy said yes.

Jason looked at his wife and they started to laugh. The technician began to laugh as well.

"Well, it's okay if you can't decide. It's a little early, and I can't be sure yet. Maybe you'll have it settled in time for the next appointment."

Sandy was more concerned with how the baby was doing.

"Does everything look okay?"

"I'm not *supposed* to say anything before the doctor looks at it and fills you in, but I don't see anything to worry about."

The technician finished and cleaned Sandy up.

"You guys can follow me. I'll take you to a room where you'll see the doctor."

****

The doctor confirmed what the tech told them, and Jason left the doctor's office to go back to the station. He promised Sandy he'd be home for dinner.

When he arrived on the third floor, Vanessa was there reading from a file. Her feet on the desk, she was leaning back in her chair.

"How was the ultrasound?"

"Good. Everything looks fine."

"Did you find out the sex?"

"No." Jason laughed remembering the scene at the doctor's office. "It was too early. Sandy and I can't decide if we *want* to know."

"Knowing makes the shopping and preparation a lot easier."

"Yeah. I don't really care if we know, so I'll leave it up to Sandy."

Vanessa threw the file on desk.

"I ran a records check on the manager, owner, and gardener at Orchid Village."

Jason sat down across from her at his desk.

"Come up with anything?"

"The owner and manager are clean, just parking tickets. The gardener is another story. He was arrested two years ago for peeping in windows at Orchid Village."

"Really? That would explain his defensiveness."

"The charges were dropped and, obviously, he kept his job."

"Still, seems like something worth following up. What about our victim from earlier today?"

"He arrived at the morgue about an hour ago. Doc Davis said he would have something for us in the morning."

Jason stood back up.

"Good. Since we don't have anything urgent, I told Sandy I'd be home for dinner, so I'm out of here. See ya in the morning?"

"Yup. Rob said the baby would be in bed when I got home, and he has a steak with my name on it."

"Enjoy." The elevator opened and Jason stepped in. "Goodnight."

****

He sat in his car watching the front door. The next target was on the third floor, which made it more difficult to get in and get out. Planning was imperative, and he'd watched carefully to gain the information he needed.

He'd learned when the target went to bed, when the target got up, and if the target had visitors during the evening. All were important factors in deciding what time to make his move.

Fortunately, most retirees keep better schedules than a New York subway. They're creatures of habit. They eat at same time, go to sleep at the same time, wake at the same time. So far, things had worked out perfectly. A few more and he'll be finished.

It's not that he disliked the retirees, but they were pawns in a bigger game, one he had to win.

Right on schedule, the target got off the elevator and walked to their apartment door. If the target stayed true to the pattern, the lights would go out in less than forty-five minutes, and there wouldn't be movement again until well after midnight.

He looked at his watch. Seven-thirty. He'd have a four-hour window to make his move.

Chapter 8

Jason's phone began to vibrate on his way into work the next morning.

"Hello."

"Good morning," Vanessa chirped. "You on your way?"

"Yeah, five minutes out. What's up?"

"The lieutenant caught me as soon as I got here. There was an attempted break-in at Orchid Village last night."

"Attempted?"

"Yeah. You remember Willie Davis, the black man who found our first victim's body?"

"Sure."

"He was up about eleven-thirty and spotted someone trying to cut his door chain. He yelled at them and they took off."

"Did he get a look at the person?"

"I don't know. You want to go see him?"

"Yes. I'm pulling into the parking lot now; do you want to meet me out here?"

"Be right down."

****

Vanessa had called Willie Davis while they were on the way out to Orchid Village. He told her he was at the community center with Grace and Ruby.

The detectives parked and went in to find the group huddled together in the reading room. The look on their faces said it all. They were terrified.

Jason came up behind Willie and laid his hand on his shoulder.

"Good morning. Can we join you?"

The ladies nodded and Willie pulled out the chair next to him.

"By all means."

Vanessa stayed standing, as was their habit. One detective sitting and one standing, looking over everything. Willie offered Vanessa a chair.

"You're welcome to join us, Detective Layne."

She smiled. "Thanks, Willie. I'm fine standing."

Ruby perked up. "That's my Bill, always a gentleman."

Willie gave her a smile and touched her arm.

Grace looked at Jason. "Willie was just telling us about last night."

Jason kept the mood light. "Oh good, perfect timing. Okay if we listen in?"

Jason could see Willie appreciated what Jason was doing. The women were afraid, and there was no sense in making it worse. Willie took it a step further.

"Shouldn't we go to the apartment so I can show you what happened?"

Jason nodded. "Actually, that's a very good idea."

Willie got up and smiled at the ladies. "I'll talk to you two later."

****

Once Jason and Vanessa were in the apartment with Willie, he went over the events of the night before.

"I had dinner with Ruby and Grace. Ruby makes an awesome chili, but I always pay for it later. Anyway, about ten-thirty, I got up to get some antacid for my stomach."

Willie walked through the events as he spoke.

"I was walking out of my room, toward the kitchen, when I noticed the door ajar. A set of bolt-cutters comes through the opening, so I yelled, and the cutters disappeared. I ran to the door, opened it, but didn't see anyone."

When he was done, Vanessa peppered him with questions.

"You said you saw a set of bolt cutters coming through the crack in the door?"

"That's what they looked like."

"Would you normally be awake at the time you surprised the intruder?"

Willie thought about it for a minute.

"No, I guess not. My reflux was acting up, or I probably would've been asleep."

"Could you tell which way the intruder went?"

Willie went to the door and opened it. Stepping outside with the detectives, he pointed at a stairwell leading down the back of the building.

"It sounded like he went down those stairs."

Jason headed for the stairwell while Vanessa said goodbye. She caught up with him at the bottom.

"Find anything?"

"No. Too many footprints to be of any use, but I'd bet he went upstairs from here, as well as coming back down." He waved his hand in the air. "No security cameras on the stairs."

Vanessa agreed, and had a theory of her own to offer up.

"The locks weren't damaged, and our guy brought cutters with him. I think he knew there was a chain, and I think he knew Willie's habits."

"Which means you think Willie was stalked?"

"It fits." Vanessa's phone began to vibrate. "Detective Layne."

"Vanessa, this is Patton."

"Yes, sir. What's up?"

"Where are you two?"

"Orchid Village. We just finished talking to Willie Davis, the man whose apartment was broken into last night."

"I just took a call at Jason's desk. It came from a Tonya Jensen."

Vanessa shot Jason a look. She recognized Tabby's real name.

"She said a neighbor of Fred Murphy called, saying there's a smell coming from Mr. Murphy's apartment, and the neighbor knew Mrs. Jensen has a key and wants her to check it out."

"That's right. She has all of her friends' keys."

"Well, Mrs. Jensen called because she's afraid to go in the apartment alone. She wanted to know if Jason could go in for her. Can you two get over there?"

"Yes. We're on our way."

Vanessa hung up and started for the car. Jason was right beside her.

"What's up?"

"Wasn't Fred Murphy the member of Willie Davis's group who was on vacation in Florida?"

"Yeah."

"Tabby Jensen got a call to check on a smell coming from the apartment. She's too scared to go in."

They got to the car and took off for Fred Murphy's building.

****

Fred Murphy lived in a second-story apartment. Tabby Jensen was waiting by the elevator.

"Thank you for coming, Detective Strong."

"No problem, Tabby. What's up?"

"Fred's next-door neighbor called me. She smelled something, and thought Fred might have left some trash out before going on vacation. When I went to check, the smell was too strong. I don't think it's garbage."

"Okay, Tabby. Do you have the key?"

"Yes." She handed the key ring to Jason, showing him which one.

"Thank you. You stay here while we go check."

"Okay."

Jason and Vanessa took the stairs to the second floor and turned left, toward Fred Murphy's apartment. They were still a couple doors away when Jason smelled it. Vanessa covered her nose with her hand.

Once a detective has smelled a decomposing body, there's never any doubt what they're about to find when they come across another.

Jason put the key in the door and opened it. He was immediately struck with the combination of rotting flesh and ice-cold air. The A/C had been left on very cold in this apartment. No doubt to cover what was likely a dead body.

Jason found a light switch on the entry wall and flipped it on. He could see the living room and kitchen from the door, but nothing appeared out of the ordinary.

They moved to the hall and the odor became overpowering. Jason put his sleeve across his face, stepped into the first bedroom, and found the light switch.

The light came on to expose a horror show. What Jason assumed to be Fred Murphy's body lay on the bed, covered in flies. He saw the strip of tape, loose now, and a bag by the head.

He stepped back and closed the door. Vanessa was following him, but hadn't seen the body.

"Is he in there?"

Jason did his best to keep from throwing up.

"Yeah, he's in there."

****

Back outside, Vanessa called in the murder while Jason went down to speak with Tabby. She was right where they'd left her.

"Did you find the smell?"

"Yes, I did."

"Was it rotting food?"

"No. Come sit down over here, Tabby."

The little woman started visibly shaking, as Jason escorted her to a nearby bench. When she was settled, he sat next to her and looked into her eyes.

"I'm sorry to tell you this Tabby, but Mr. Murphy is dead."

Tears started down her face.

"Was he murdered?"

"It looks like it."

She leaned toward Jason and let her tears flow. Jason put an arm around her and waited. He wasn't going anywhere until this little lady was okay.

Vanessa came over a few minutes later. "I called it in. The forensic teams are on their way."

At the sound of Vanessa's voice, Tabby sat up. "I need to tell Willie and the others."

A voice came from behind them. "Tell Willie what?"

The elderly man walked up, smiling.

"I saw you two detectives take off like bats out of you-know-where, so I followed you over here. What's going on?"

Vanessa rested her hand on Willie's shoulder. "It's about your friend, Fred Murphy."

"What about him? He was surprising his granddaughter at her graduation. Did he have an accident?"

Tabby stood up and moved toward her friend. "Fred never made it to Florida, Willie. He died in his apartment."

Willie looked from one face to another, then up toward the door of Fred's unit, and finally back at Vanessa. "What happened?"

"Same as Ruth."

Willie shook his head, turned, and walked away. Tabby called after him. "Where are you going, Willie?"

"I need a few minutes."

Jason stood up next to Tabby. "Let him go."

Tabby nodded, and Jason took her arm, getting her to sit back down. "Tabby, we need to know a few things."

Again, she nodded, still looking toward Willie, who had stopped next to the pool building.

"When was Fred supposed to leave for Florida?"

"Three weeks ago. He was flying out on a Wednesday but wasn't sure when he would be back."

"Did he have family expecting him?"

"No. He said he was surprising his granddaughter at her college graduation."

Vanessa had taken out her pad and was making notes.

Jason continued. "You said it was a Wednesday when he left. Do you know the date?"

"Not exactly, but I'm sure it's on my calendar. I know it was a Wednesday because he missed our card game that night."

Willie had walked back over to the group.

"Somebody needs to tell Grace and Ruby."

Jason stood. "Vanessa and I will go there now. We need to speak with them, anyway. Willie, can you take care of Tabby?"

"Of course."

Chapter 9

Jason knocked twice and stepped back. Vanessa was looking at her notes from the last time they had spoken to the two sisters.

"Ruby! Get the door, please."

Jason and Vanessa smiled at each other. Even through the door, the yelling was loud.

There was no response but a minute later, the door opened.

Ruby, dressed in a smock and wearing fuzzy slippers, looked at them with sleepy eyes. "Can I help you?"

"Mrs. Pryor, I'm Detective Strong and this is my partner, Detective Layne. Do you remember speaking with us the other night?"

Ruby rubbed her eyes. "Yes, of course. Is there something wrong?"

"We need to speak to you and your sister."

"Okay, come in."

As Jason and Vanessa followed Ruby into the apartment, Jason nodded toward his partner to take the lead.

Vanessa took the seat offered by Ruby, while Jason leaned against the half-wall separating the living room and kitchen. The apartment was small but neat. Actually, Jason thought the furniture made it smaller than it was. Large, flower-patterned, overstuffed chairs and a matching couch with doilies over the arms, made the place feel cramped

Grace appeared from one of the bedrooms adjoined to the living room and didn't need a re-introduction.

"Detectives, hello."

Ruby sat on the couch across from Vanessa, and Grace joined her. The resemblance was obvious. Jason knew Vanessa had been worrying about the sisters, and it was obvious when she spoke to them.

"How are you two doing?"

Grace smiled at the female detective. "Still a little shook up, but okay considering. Thank you for asking."

Vanessa didn't return the smile. "I'm afraid we have some bad news…"

Both ladies seemed to freeze, afraid of what would come next.

"…Fred Murphy had been found dead."

Grace looked confused. "In Florida?"

"No, here. He never made it to Florida."

Both women began to cry, and Ruby tucked her knees in toward her chest, curling into a fetal position. Grace fought for composure.

"Was he…killed?"

"It appears so."

Grace sat back against the couch. "Merciful heaven!"

"Do Tabby and Willie know?"

"Yes. We've talked with both of them."

Jason came across the room, crouched down, and looked directly at both women.

"As tough as this is, we need to ask you a few questions."

Ruby looked like a scared little girl despite her age, and Jason's heart broke for both of them.

Grace nodded. "We understand."

"Did you two hear about Darrel Patterson?"

Ruby appeared to have shut down. Grace answered all the questions.

"Yes, we heard."

"Did either of you know Mr. Patterson?"

"Yes. We'd run into him at the rent meetings."

Vanessa looked puzzled. "Rent meetings? I thought all of these units were condos."

Grace nodded her head. "They are. That is, all except the ones grandfathered in from the early days, when the complex was a rental property."

"Are you two renters?"

Grace nodded.

Jason made a mental note to ask Steve Jaffe about the history of the complex. "Did either of you ever see Mr. Patterson argue with anyone at those meetings?"

Grace shook her head. "Not that I remember. For the most part, the meetings are not contentious. Just information for the few of us left renting."

"What about your friends? Did they have anyone who might be angry with them?"

Again, Grace shook her head, before looking at Jason. "Do you have any idea who might be behind this?"

"We have people we're looking at, but that's all," Jason stood. "Thank you for your help."

Vanessa and Grace got up at the same time, but Ruby remained curled on the couch.

They walked to the door, but before they left, Jason turned and looked at both ladies. "Be careful."

Grace gave them a sad smile. "We will."

****

The next morning, Jason met Vanessa in the elevator heading up to their desks. She carried a forensic report in her hand.

He pointed at the papers. "Been to the basement, I see."

"I wanted a look at the forensic report before we go out to the Village."

"My thought exactly."

They got off at the third floor and went to their desks. The lieutenant's office door was closed, but it only muffled the fact someone was very angry.

Jason gave Vanessa a 'what's up?' look. She just shrugged.

They had just flipped open the forensic file when the door burst open and an elderly man came marching out of the office. Tall, nicely dressed, his face beet red, he flew past the detectives. He went straight to the stairs, not waiting for the elevator.

The lieutenant was sitting at his desk, looking at the ceiling, his face a similar color to the man who had just left. He noticed the two detectives watching him.

"You two, get in here."

They went into the lieutenant's office. When they had closed the door behind them, he tossed a newspaper across the desk.

"I had this delivered to me today. The man you just saw leave was the delivery boy."

Jason looked at the headline.

POLICE SEARCHING FOR THE ORCHID VILLAGE CONDO KILLER

Jason's friend and nemesis, Devin James, had written the front-page article. A senior writer with the San Antonio News, James had long been a thorn in Jason's side. He'd also been an asset, invaluable in solving one of Jason's toughest cases.

Vanessa read the headline aloud, finishing with a moan.

"Really? 'Condo Killer'? We're not searching for someone killing condos!"

Patton let a smile cross his lips, but he didn't like the reporter, and Jason knew it. The lieutenant held Jason, fairly or not, responsible for the reporter's actions.

"I didn't tell him a thing, Lieutenant."

"I assumed you didn't. The man who just left, do you know who he is?"

"No."

"His name is George Weber. He's president of the condo board at Orchid Village, and as you could no doubt tell, he isn't happy."

"What's his problem?"

"The usual. He thinks we're not doing enough, and what we are doing, isn't being done fast enough. Where are we on the investigation?"

"Not much to go on. We think it's someone who's a regular at the Village and doesn't seem out of place. We've run background on all employees."

"And?"

Vanessa piped up. "Everyone comes back clean except the head gardener. He has an arrest for peeping, but the charges were dropped."

"Well, let's go at him hard. See if you can shake something loose. Anything else?"

"We haven't interviewed the owner, because he's been out of town, which is also his alibi."

"Okay, we need to strong on this. I want you two all over Orchid Village. At least we can let this sucker know we're serious about finding him."

"Yes sir," they said in unison.

Tied to Murder

The heat had just turned from simmer to boiling with the discovery of a third body. Summer was hot in West Texas, but not nearly as hot as working in Homicide when people were dying.

****

As Jason drove, Vanessa read from the forensic report. Most of it they already knew, but she did see something interesting.

"The tape found on the man in the river is a generic match to the tape used on Mrs. Rogers. The method of restraint is the same in all three cases."

Something was bugging Jason.

"Why do you suppose the killer took the first victim away from the complex, but the not the others?"

Vanessa thought about it. "Maybe he was nearly caught the first time, and decided removing them wasn't worth the risk."

Jason wasn't convinced. "Maybe."

They arrived at the office of Orchid Village to find a silver Cadillac CTS parked in an employee spot. Jason saw it first.

"Maybe the owner is finally back in town."

They got out and went inside. Somebody was yelling in the manager's office. "Then find out!"

Jason stuck his head in the door. "Are we interrupting something?"

Steve Jaffe looked up from his desk. The man who had been doing the yelling turned toward Jason, annoyed at being interrupted.

"Can we help you?"

Steve Jaffe cleared his throat. "Marcus, these are the two detectives I was telling you about."

Marcus Winston immediately dialed down his temper.

"Oh." He extended his hand. "Marcus Winston."

Jason sized him up as he shook his hand. Medium build, less than six feet tall, receding gray hair. Jason guessed him to be in his early sixties.

"Detective Jason Strong." he nodded over his shoulder. "That's my partner, Detective Layne."

Winston nodded at her. "Detective."

Jason was curious about all the yelling, but their first task was to interview the owner.

"Can we have a few minutes of your time, Mr. Winston?"

"Of course. Let's go back to the break room."

Jason and Vanessa followed Marcus Winston back to the same place where they had met the gardening crew. The two men each grabbed a chair while Vanessa pulled out her notebook, and leaned against the wall.

Jason started the questioning. "Mr. Winston…"

"Marcus, please."

"…Marcus. I gather you're familiar with the deaths in your complex?"

"Of course. It's terrible. Have you got any leads?"

Jason ignored the question and pushed forward with his own.

"Your manager told us you were out of town when each of the deaths occurred."

"That's right. I'm building another complex in Austin, and I'm gone a lot of the time."

"And is there someone who can verify you being there?"

Marcus Winston hesitated before answering. "Am I a suspect?"

"No, just routine procedure."

The owner looked skeptical, but answered the question. "Yes, my secretary."

Vanessa jumped in. "Her name?"

"Norma…Norma Waters."

"And the phone number?"

"It's my office number. 555-0956."

Vanessa wrote it down.

Jason watched Marcus as he spoke. There was no reason to suspect this man of such ugly crimes, but Jason felt he was holding something back. "Do you have any idea why these people in your community would be targeted?"

Marcus shook his head in apparent disbelief. "I can't imagine why anyone would want to hurt these elderly folks."

Jason stood up, indicating they were done. Marcus stood up with him and they shook hands.

As the detectives left, they passed Steve Jaffe, still at his desk. Jason noticed something he hadn't seen previously. A cowboy hat hung on a hook behind the manager.

"That your hat, Steve?"

"Yeah, I got used to wearing them on the family farm. Never really gave it up."

"No kidding. Ever rope a calf?"

Steve looked confused. "Well, sure. I grew up on a cattle farm. Why?"

"Just curious. Do you know where I can find Jose Jimenez?"

"Yeah, I believe he's mowing by the back gate of the property."

"Okay, thanks."

Steve stood up. "Jason?"

"Yeah?"

"Do you know when they'll release the two apartments being held as crime scenes?"

"No, I don't. I'll find out and let you know."

"Thanks, I appreciate it."

The detectives left and got in their car. Jason told Vanessa about his conversation with Steve Jaffe.

She was intrigued, but skeptical. "A lot of people in this part of the country grew up on cattle farms."

"True."

Driving to the rear of the complex, they spotted Jose riding a large mower. They parked by the curb and walked over to stand in the path of the head gardener. For a moment, Jason wasn't sure Jose was going to stop.

Finally, he idled the mower, glaring at the detectives. "What?"

Jason could barely hear over the mower. He gestured for Jose to shut it down.

The gardener let it run for a minute longer, before reaching down, and shutting the mower off. He repeated his question. "What?"

Jason was prepared this time for the gardener's attitude.

"We've been looking into your past, Jose. It seems you had a run-in with the law a few years ago."

The gardener leapt off the mower, causing Vanessa to take a step back. Jason didn't move.

"The charges were dropped! I was innocent!"

Jason kept his voice level. "Still, considering what the charges were, and looking at what's going on around here, you make a pretty good suspect to me."

The lieutenant wanted them to stir things up, and Jason figured making Jose nervous would do the trick.

"I got nothin' to do with those people dyin'! Nothin,' you hear?"

Jason shook his head, a concerned look on his face. "I don't know, Jose. You're not giving me an alibi, and you're not helping yourself by coming up with some information for me. You wouldn't answer any of my questions the other day. I figure, a guy in your position would rather cooperate than make himself look bad."

The gardener was clearly flustered, but he stuck to his story. "I don't know nothin.' I wasn't around when those folks died. I was at home."

Jason wasn't sure if the gardener was lying, but he wanted Jose to think he was suspicious of him.

"Okay, Jose." He shook his head doubtfully. "We'll be in touch."

The gardener climbed back onto the mower as Jason and Vanessa walked back to their car. Vanessa let out a chuckle.

"I wasn't sure he was going to stop the mower before hitting us."

"I know! I thought we were going to be 'mowed down'! Get it mowed..."

Vanessa rolled her eyes. "I get it. So, do you think we ruffled his feathers?"

"I'd say so. I just hope it makes him nervous enough to give us something."

Chapter 10

They arrived back at the station in the late afternoon.

Jason wanted to verify Marcus Winston's alibi. He dialed the number the condo owner had given Vanessa.

"Hello?"

Jason noticed the informal answering of the phone. "Norma Waters?"

"Yes. Who's calling?"

"Ms. Waters, my name's Detective Jason Strong. I'm with the San Antonio Police Department."

"Yes, Detective. Marcus said you might call."

"Ms. Waters…"

"Please, call me Norma."

"…Norma, are you in the construction office at this time?"

There was a pause before she answered. "Uh, no. Why?"

"I hoped you could look at the office calendar, and verify whether Mr. Winston was in Austin on the dates in question."

"He gave me the dates you were interested in, and I was able to confirm he was here."

Jason didn't like the feel of this conversation at all. Something wasn't right.

"He was there on all of the dates?"

"Yes. All of them."

"Okay, I appreciate your time. I won't bother you further."

"No bother, Detective. Goodbye."

The phone clicked in Jason's ear, and he looked up to see Vanessa watching him. "She verified he was there?"

Jason put the phone down. "She did, but there's something not kosher about her statement."

"How so?"

"Didn't Winston say he gave us the office number to call Norma Waters?"

"I believe so, why?"

"She answered it like it was a personal phone. And said she wasn't at the office."

Lieutenant Patton called them into his office, interrupting Jason. "How did it go out there today?"

Jason brought the lieutenant up to speed, and when he was done, John Patton stood up. He grabbed a cloth, and as he spoke, he erased the whiteboard at the end of his office. "Patrols have been increased through the complex, and they've been told to be very visible, using spotlights, etc."

He turned and looked at Vanessa. "Okay, let's put this case on the board and see what it looks like. Give me the names of the deceased in order of discovery."

Vanessa listed them off. Ruth Rogers, Darrel Patterson, and Fred Murphy. The lieutenant wrote them down. Without turning around, he asked for the next piece of information.

"Cause of death in each?"

"Same," Jason answered. "Suffocation by a plastic bag taped over their heads."

"And no sign of a sexual attack?"

"None."

The lieutenant rubbed his hand across the top of his head.

"Okay, let's see if there are any lines to be drawn between these victims, besides where they lived and how they died."

Vanessa, as was her habit, raised her hand to speak. Despite the stress he was under, John Patton smiled. "Yes, Ms. Layne?"

She smiled back. "I think we should add the name of Willie Davis. He wasn't killed, but he was targeted, and any connection of the cases would probably include him as well."

To signify he agreed, John Patton wrote the elderly man's name on the board.

"Okay," he said. "Let's start with demographics. They're all elderly, but that doesn't set them apart from the rest of the community. It may, however, be tied to the motive."

Jason copied the notes on the board into his notebook as the lieutenant continued. "Neither race nor gender seem to be significant, since they vary from victim to victim. Three men, one woman. One black, three white." He rubbed his head again. "What about location? Are they all from the same building?"

Jason got out his map of Orchid Village.

"Two of the victims lived on the same cul-de-sac, but Patterson and Davis both live on different streets, on the opposite side of the complex."

"What else? Were they all friends, acquaintances, enemies?"

"Two of the victims were friends, and knew Willie Davis, but Darrel Patterson was not part of their circle."

"What about money? Were they wealthy?"

Vanessa shook her head. "Hardly. In fact, Patterson was renting his unit."

The lieutenant dropped heavily into his chair.

"Renting? I thought those were condos?"

Vanessa nodded. "So did we, but Grace Caldwell said they were rentals before they were turned into condominiums. She's a renter, too."

"And the other victims? Were they renting?"

Jason and Vanessa looked at each other. Jason had meant to talk to Steve Jaffe about the history of the complex, but hadn't got around to it yet. They didn't know if the other victims were renters.

They both shrugged.

John Patton rolled his eyes. "Well, let's find out. It's mighty thin, but it's all we've got right now. Keep me informed."

The meeting was over. They stood to leave when Jason remembered Steve Jaffe's request.

"The manager out at Orchid Village asked if we could release the two units we're holding as crime scenes."

The lieutenant thought for a moment. "Not sure. I'll check with Doc Josie."

****

Once outside the office, Jason and Vanessa looked over their notes. Neither one could find a notation about the status of the other apartments. Vanessa offered to call Steve Jaffe, but Jason said no.

"I want to go see him in person. We'll go first thing in the morning."

"Actually, you mind making the trip solo?"

"Why? What's up?"

"I've got to take my little man for his check-up in the morning."

"Sure, no problem."

She elbowed him in the side. "You'll be doing the same thing soon!"

He laughed. He was looking forward to it.

Chapter 11

Unlocking the door to her apartment, Tabby went inside and began her normal routine.

First, lock the door handle. Next, turn both deadbolts, one near the top and one near the bottom of the door. Finally, run the chain across the doorframe.

She set her purse down on the table by the door and walked across the living room to the patio door. Pulling back the curtain, she made sure the door was still locked, and the metal pin through the frame was in place.

Satisfied, she went into the kitchen to make a cup of tea. The group had gotten together for the first time since Ruth and Fred were found murdered. They tried to keep things light, but it was more about being in each other's company than it was about cards.

Tabby felt they needed to meet, resume a routine of some sort, and not stay locked up in their own apartments. She didn't have trouble convincing Willie or Ruby, but Grace had been reluctant. Finally, she had given in to Tabby's gentle insistence that getting out was for the best.

The teakettle whistled and she reached for a cup. Something came to her nose. A smell.

What is that?

She made her tea, no cream with light sugar, before going and sitting in her favorite chair. She couldn't put her finger on why the smell was so familiar.

Putting it out of her mind, she sipped the tea, before picking up her needlepoint and going back to stitching the Golden Retriever embroidery she was currently working on.

Getting lost in her hobby, she never heard a thing.

A hand reached around her face, slapping a piece of duct tape over her mouth. Before she could move, a rope looped twice around her and her chair. It pulled tight and she was unable to move.

Panic gripped her as she tried to turn and see who was behind her. Before she could see him, a bag dropped down over her head, and everything went dark.

In an odd moment of calm before she died, Tabby recognized that smell, and knew who her murderer was.

****

Wednesday morning, Jason drove directly out to Orchid Village from home. Steve Jaffe had been out of town for several days, and Jason was anxious to talk to him. He found the manager in his office.

"Morning, Steve."

Steve looked up from his desk and, seeing Jason, stood.

"Detective." They shook hands. "Any news?"

Steve gestured at a chair in front of his desk as he sat back down. Jason pulled his notebook and took the seat. "No news, but I do have more questions."

Steve leaned back, apparently unconcerned. "Shoot."

"Can you tell me the history of Orchid Village?"

Steve looked puzzled. "History?"

"Yeah. We understand the Village was a rental community at one time?"

"Oh, that. I didn't know what you were referring to." He sat forward. "Yeah, it's true. When Marcus started construction on the complex, things were good as far as real estate was concerned. He was nearing completion of the early phases when the Texas market, like the rest of the country, went down the drain."

Jason remembered how bad things had gotten for folks during that time. Texas, California, Arizona, as well as Florida, were particularly hard hit.

Steve continued. "Anyway, the bank was going to close out the construction loan, cut its losses, but that would've left Marcus bankrupt. City leaders didn't want a white elephant on the San Antonio landscape either, so they and Marcus convinced the bank to continue the financing by converting the units to rentals."

Jason made several notes. "When did the complex transition to condos?"

"About seven years ago."

"And how was that handled?"

Steve reached behind him and pulled a piece of paper from the file cabinet. He slid it across the desk to Jason. "This letter was sent out to each renter."

Jason took the letter and scanned it. The note, on Orchid Village letterhead, proclaimed the exciting news of the transition to condos. Each resident had the opportunity to purchase his or her unit. The letter continued with financing options and other details, which Jason skipped over.

Marcus Winston's signature ran across the bottom.

Jason tried to imagine getting a letter like this in his mailbox. He looked up at Steve, who was watching him. "How did people react?"

"The response was overwhelmingly positive. These units were fairly expensive rentals to begin with, and most could afford to buy their unit. The main draw to the Village had been the amenities."

"Was there anyone who was a particular problem? Someone who might have a grudge?"

Steve didn't answer right away, and Jason could tell the manager was running the events of that time through his mind. Finally, he shook his head.

"No, no one comes to mind that was really angry. You have to understand, people under lease were allowed either to remain in their units until they bought them, or the unit was vacated. Nobody was forced out. That's why some of the units are still rentals."

"Can I keep this letter?"

Steve nodded. "Of course."

Jason folded it and put in his pocket. "One other thing. Can I get a list of the remaining units under lease, and the names of the people renting them?"

Steve stood up and moved to a cabinet across the room. He pulled out a single sheet of paper and handed it to Jason. The list was short, probably less than ten names.

Jason raised an eyebrow. "Not many left?"

"No, just a handful."

Jason quickly looked over the list and spotted the names of Ruth Rogers, Fred Murphy, Darrel Patterson, and Willie Davis. He'd just found the link connecting the victims, and Jason bet the motive was somehow tied to the same list.

Jason held up the list. "Keep this, too?"

"Of course. Anything else? I need to make my rounds."

Jason extended his hand and they shook. .

"No, and thanks again."

He needed to call Vanessa. She should be back from the doctor appointment by now.

****

Jason never got the chance to dial his partner. She called him before he got to his car. "Hi, partner." He sensed urgency in her voice.

"Hi. You still at Orchid Village?"

Jason began to hear sirens, and the hair on the back of his neck stood up. "Yeah. Why?"

"We've got another one. I'm on my way."

Jason watched a couple black-and-whites, lights flashing, turn down one of the side lanes in the complex. "Do you have a name?"

"Tonya Jensen."

His heart sank as he pulled out the renters list, already knowing the answer. There she was, Tonya Jensen, third name down. "I was afraid of that."

"Afraid of what?"

"I'll explain when you get here."

He hung up and sprinted after the lights.

Chapter 12

When Jason got to the apartment, he found Willie Davis standing with an officer. Just coming out of the apartment was another officer, who walked over to Jason.

"There's an elderly lady in there. I checked for a pulse, but she's gone. We didn't touch anything else."

Jason nodded. "Okay. Who found the body?"

"The elderly man talking to Officer Cain." The uniform fumbled for his notebook. "The man's name is…"

"Willie Davis. I'm familiar with him. Create a perimeter, you know the drill."

"Yes, sir."

Jason walked toward the open apartment door, nodding at Willie, but not stopping to talk to him. He found it odd Willie had now found two victims, and suffered the only attack that *didn't* succeed.

Jason entered the apartment and took the few minutes before forensics and the coroner showed up to get an untouched feel for the situation.

He found Tabby in a chair, bag over her head and tape around her neck. Apparently, she had been doing some sort of a craft project when she was ambushed. It lay on the floor by her feet.

As he came around in front of the tiny woman, he began to shake uncontrollably. Anger took hold of him in a way he'd never felt before. *How could someone be so cruel to someone so defenseless?*

Jason knew suffocation was a cruel death, and the fear Tabby must have felt as her life ebbed away made him shake even more. If he had the killer here now, he could choke the life out of him with his bare hands.

Jason struggled to get himself under control. He was not normally emotional at crime scenes, and it would serve Tabby no good for him to lose his composure.

He left her as she was and moved to the patio door. It was locked, and had a metal pin through the frame. Definitely not the point of entry. Checking every window in the small unit, he found them all locked.

Back at the front door, he met Vanessa coming in.

"What have we got?" she asked.

Jason filled her in without meeting her gaze. He was checking the front door locks, but also hiding his anger. "Same method. She was probably surprised from behind while sitting in the chair."

"Point of entry?"

"Nothing unlocked anywhere. Everything here looks untouched, as well." He gestured toward the multiple locks and chain on the door.

Vanessa's face scrunched up as she peered at the doorjamb. "No sign of prying. So, our guy was either let in by Tabby, or was inside when she got home."

"That's what I think."

They moved out of the doorway to let the forensic and med-tech folks in. The apartment began to swarm with personnel, so Jason went outside, followed by Vanessa.

"Who found the body?" she asked.

"Willie Davis."

"Again?"

"That's right. Bad luck, coincidence, or something else?"

Jason could tell which one Vanessa considered likely by her reaction.

"Poor Willie!"

Jason followed Vanessa over to where the elderly man stood, still giving his statement to Officer Cain.

Willie tried a half-smile as he saw the detectives walk up, but it was in vain. He appeared to be in shock. Vanessa touched the old man on the shoulder. "Willie, you okay?"

Jason nodded at him, but didn't get between Vanessa and Willie. He stood back, watching as Vanessa asked Willie to go over the story again.

"I called Tabby this morning just to check up on her, but couldn't get an answer. I tried again around eleven this morning, and still couldn't get her, so I came over."

"You have a key?"

"Yes. Since Ruth and Fred, we've all had each other's keys."

"Wasn't the chain on?" It was Jason, and he didn't hide his anger very well.

Willie glanced toward Jason before answering. "No. That's when I knew something was wrong. Tabby never left the chain off."

Vanessa looked at the officer and he indicated he was done. Vanessa steered Willie to a nearby bench and sat beside him. "Have you reached Grace and Ruby?"

"No, not yet."

"Well, it's okay to go. When you feel up to it, you can go see them."

"Thank you."

When Vanessa looked up, Jason was still standing, watching them. She got up and walked over to him. "You don't seriously think that old man is capable of these crimes?"

Jason realized his anger might be affecting his judgment, but everyone needed to be looked at.

"Probably not, but we can't rule anyone out yet."

Vanessa gave him a sideways look, and Jason was grateful when she changed the subject. "What was it you said you would tell me when I got out here?"

Jason recalled the list and pulled the paper out of his pocket.

"This is a list of the remaining rental units and their occupants. Every one of our victims is on it."

Vanessa took the paper and studied it. "Has to be the connection, but why?"

"I don't know, but Willie is on that list, along with Grace and Ruby, and others we haven't met yet."

Jason's phone rang. "Strong."

"Jason, this is Patton. What have you got?"

"A fourth victim. Same method."

Jason heard the lieutenant let out a long sigh. "Crap!"

"That's one word for it."

"Okay. Listen, you can tell the manager they can have the Patterson apartment, but not the others. Forensics said the Patterson unit is not considered the primary crime scene, and they're done with it."

"Okay."

"Get with me when you two are back from the scene. George Weber was back in this morning."

"Great." Jason rolled his eyes at Vanessa. "We'll see you then."

Jason hung up and Vanessa gave him an inquiring look.

"Weber, the condo board guy, was in to see the lieutenant."

Vanessa waved the list at Jason. "You want to go visit the rest of the people on this list?"

"Seems like a good idea. Who's up first?"

Chapter 13

They finished interviewing the last person on the list and Jason looked at his watch. Nearly four.

"We need to get back to the station and meet with the lieutenant."

Their interviews with the other people on the list hadn't produced any new leads. They'd left each one with the same warning. 'Be careful.'

Vanessa had driven them around the complex, and now she dropped Jason at the office. "See you at the station?"

He nodded. "Yeah. I'm gonna go in and tell Steve he can have the Patterson unit."

"Okay."

She drove off as Jason went into the office. "Steve?"

"Back here." Steve came out to meet Jason.

"My lieutenant said you can have the Patterson unit. The other two need to stay closed up for now."

"Okay, thanks. It'll make Marcus happy."

"You have a waiting list or something for those units?"

"Actually, yes. Ever since we converted."

"How much one of those units bring?"

"Around a hundred-fifty."

"Thousand?"

"Yup."

Jason was amazed. He knew the market had rebounded, but that was a lot of money. He said goodbye and headed out to his car. It didn't take long to do the math.

Four available units totaled over a half-million dollars in revenue. That was what he called a motive.

He got in his car and drove back to the station. When he got up to the third floor, Vanessa was working at her desk. Jason dropped in his chair. "Guess what I just found out from Steve Jaffe?"

She looked up from her computer. "Guess what I just found out about Willie Davis?"

Jason smiled. "Me first."

She nodded and sat back, folding her arms across her chest.

"Each one of the units that comes up for sale, after they are vacated by one of the renters, goes for more than a hundred-fifty."

"Thousand?"

Jason was nodding. "That's what I said! Yeah, a hundred-fifty thousand."

"Wow! That's a lot of incentive to open up units."

"I know, right? What's your news?"

Vanessa looked back down at her computer. "Well, I thought I would prove you wrong on your suspicion of Willie Davis, so I looked into his past."

"And?"

"He grew up on a Colorado cattle ranch."

"Really?"

"Yes."

Jason could tell she was disappointed. He could also see she still didn't believe Willie could be responsible for the deaths.

The lieutenant's door opened and he called them into his office. He waited for Jason to sit. "What's the status of the Orchid Village case?"

Jason pulled out the list of rental units.

"We found a connection between the victims. Your hunch was correct. All of the victims lived in rentals left over from the conversion to condos."

As was his habit, John Patton rubbed his face with both hands, thinking while stressing.

"Well, that explains the comment from the condo board president. He said something to the effect of 'the renters are a problem that hurts our property values.'"

Vanessa grunted. "Class act!"

The lieutenant rolled his eyes. "You have no idea."

Jason continued. "There's another less obvious connection. The victims all knew each other from the rent meetings, but I tend to think it strengthens the first connection."

The lieutenant got up and went to the white board, erasing some of the writing from their last meeting. "Do we have a list of suspects?"

Jason looked at his notes.

"The gardener, Jose Jimenez." Patton wrote it on the board. "The complex owner, Marcus Winston, and one of the names on the rental list, Willie Davis."

Patton looked back at Jason. "The same guy on our victim list?"

Vanessa wasn't buying it. "Jason thinks Willie discovering two of the victims, and having his own close call, is suspicious. I don't see any way he could be responsible."

The lieutenant wrote the name down anyway. "Right now, I'm not ruling anybody out. Anybody else?"

"Just the complex manager, Steve Jaffe. He's on site most of the time, and has a ranch background."

The lieutenant wrote Jaffe's name, followed by a question mark as suspect five, and lastly, he added the name George Weber.

Vanessa and Jason spoke at the same time. "The condo board chairman?"

"Like I said, no one is ruled out." He wrote a dash next to each name. "Motive and opportunity for each?"

Vanessa pointed at the gardener's name. "He has a record of peeping, and opportunity. He also has no solid alibi."

Jason spoke about Marcus Winston. "He has an alibi, although a shaky one. He also has probably the biggest motive. Each unit will sell for over a hundred-fifty."

The lieutenant stopped and looked at the detectives. "Thousand?"

Jason and Vanessa exchanged glances before laughing. "That's what we said!"

"What's his alibi?"

"His secretary in Austin. She said he was there on each of the dates in question."

"Well, let's shake down his alibi, make sure it's solid. What about Mr. Davis?"

Jason's suspect, so he chimed in again. "He's been around each time, knows all the victims, and has a ranch background."

"Is he physically capable of doing the killings?"

Jason shrugged, but Vanessa said, "No."

"Does he have a motive? Is he angry with these people? Are they racists?"

Vanessa answered. "No, no, and no."

Jason could tell Lieutenant Patton was skeptical, but it wouldn't be first time a name appeared on a victim list, and a suspect list, at the same time.

"I just want to keep an open mind about him." Jason said.

John Patton nodded. "Fine. What about Jaffe?"

"Clean record. Job means he's been around when the killings occurred."

The lieutenant studied the board before continuing.

"Okay. The question mark obviously refers to a total unknown, someone flying under the radar." He turned and underlined the condo board chairman's name. "Vanessa, check this guy out. Let's leave no stone unturned. Any questions?"

The two detectives shook their heads.

"Good. I've got a meeting with Lieutenant Banks this afternoon, and I won't be free until tomorrow. Let's meet again in the morning."

Jason couldn't help himself. "Sarah Banks?"

"Yes, Detective. Lieutenant Sarah Banks, and don't bother asking any more questions, because you aren't getting any more answers."

They laughed and left the office.

Jason went to his desk, picking up the phone while Vanessa sat down at her computer. He punched in the number for Nina Jefferson.

"Missing Persons."

"Is Nina Jefferson in?"

"No. Who's calling?"

"Jason Strong."

"She's still in Austin, Detective. She's testifying on an old case."

"Okay, thanks."

Jason hung up and pulled out his cell phone. He had Nina in his contact list and maybe he could catch her out of court.

He pushed her number and waited.

"Hello?"

"Nina, this is Jason."

"Hi, Jason. How's things?"

"Good. Are you having fun in court?"

She grunted. "The party never stops. How's Sandy and the baby?"

"Good."

"Have you found out if it's a boy or a girl?"

Jason laughed. "Actually, we're still trying to decide if we *want* to know."

"It's a lot easier to shop when you know the sex of the baby."

"I bet. Listen, the reason I called was to ask you a favor."

"Okay, shoot."

"Do you still have contacts on the force in Austin?"

"You know I do! They all owe me big time up here." She laughed. "What do you need?"

Jason could hear her pulling up a sheet of paper. "I need to know about a man named Marcus Winston. He's got a big retirement complex under construction in Austin, called Orchid Village, and I need to know if everything is on the up and up with this guy."

"No problem. I'll make a few calls and get back to you."

"Thanks, Nina." Jason hung up.

Vanessa was watching him and waiting. "I ran a record check on the condo board guy. Nothing. Apparently, his only crime is being a jerk." She pushed a piece of paper toward Jason. "Not even a parking ticket."

Jason didn't bother to look at the paper. "Let's call it a day. See you back here in the morning?"

"Sounds good."

Chapter 14

When Jason got home, he found Sandy crying, sitting on the couch in the family room.

"Sandy, what's wrong?"

She looked at him with red eyes, tears rolling down her face. Jason sat next to her on the couch, his heart in his throat. His first thought was of their child.

"Honey, what is it? Is everything okay with the baby?"

She nodded. "It's not the baby."

Jason took a deep breath.

"It's Penny," she sobbed.

Jason's heart started pounding again.

Penny was their Great Pyrenees pup. Thick, white fur with giant eyes, she had pawed at Sandy's leg during a visit to the Humane Society, and his wife had melted. They began filling out the paperwork to adopt her immediately. She was just like a child to them. "What about her?"

"She was hit by a car," she moaned, and started crying even harder. "I'm sorry!"

Jason put his arms around his wife. "It's okay. Is she gone?"

Sandy shook her head against his shoulder. "No."

Jason pushed Sandy back so he could see her face. "Where is she?"

"At the vet. They're doing surgery to repair her leg. I just got home a few minutes ago."

Jason took another deep breath of relief. "She's gonna make it?"

Sandy nodded. "But she'll probably limp now. It was my fault."

Jason pulled her close to himself again, tighter this time. "It's okay. Tell me what happened."

She began her story, sobbing sporadically as she tried to calm down.

"I went out to get the mail and didn't make sure the door was closed behind me. She must have pawed at the door and got it open. When I got back to the house, I saw the door ajar, and turned around to see her wander into the street. The car tried to stop, but it clipped her rear-end. I didn't even stop to call anyone. The driver helped me load her up, and I took her straight to the vet."

Jason knew how attached his wife had become to their big ball of white fur. He could only imagine the guilt she was feeling, but it was still just an accident.

"Sandy, accidents happen and you know that. She's a smart dog who found her way outside. It could've just as easily happened to me."

She wiped at her face. "I heard her yelp, and she kept looking at me with those big eyes. It was awful!"

His wife's cell phone rang, and she lunged for it.

"Hello?"

Jason watched as relief washed over Sandy's face. She nodded up and down a few times, said 'thank you,' and hung up.

"The vet said she came through surgery in good shape. They're going to keep her for the night, and we can bring her home tomorrow afternoon."

"There, you see? Everything is going to be okay. We'll go get her together."

"Okay."

Jason cuddled his wife, and a thought ran through his head. If this is how they felt about their puppy, he could only imagine the impact their new baby would have on their lives.

****

The next morning, as Jason was dressing for work, his phone rang.

"This is Strong."

"Jason, it's Nina."

"Morning Nina, got something?"

"Yeah, I think. You on your way in?"

"Just about to leave."

"Okay. I'm back in town. See you when you get to the station."

He hung up and turned to see Sandy leaning in the doorway of their bedroom.

"Are you still going with me to pick up Penny?"

"Absolutely. I'll call you later with my schedule, and we'll figure out when we can meet."

She walked across the bedroom and kissed him. "Jason Strong, you're the best. I think I'll keep you."

He laughed. "Good thing, because you're not getting rid of me. You're stuck!"

He kissed her back and headed for the door.

******

When Jason arrived at the station, Vanessa was standing in doorway of Lieutenant Patton's office. She waved him over before moving in and sitting down, letting Jason take her place against the door frame. Jason found Nina Jefferson already sitting in the office.

"Hi, Nina. Morning, Lieutenant."

The lieutenant nodded. "Nina was just telling me about some investigating she did for you in Austin. I think you'll be very interested to hear what she discovered about Marcus Winston."

Jason turned toward Nina as she began to go over the story again.

"After you called, court was suspended for the day, so I decided to do some checking on your guy. I talked to three different detectives in my old precinct, and not one of them could recall encountering a Marcus Winston."

Jason began mentally crossing Winston off his suspect list. "Well, that's good I guess."

She continued. "There's more."

"Okay, shoot."

"So, I went to talk to someone I know over at City Hall. She's an old friend who works in the permits office. I asked her about Orchid Village, and she gave me a blank stare. She double-checked, but there are no permits granted for any development by that name."

Jason's mind started spinning. "Maybe they're calling it something else."

Nina shook her head. "I thought the same thing, but the only large complexes currently under construction are some downtown office buildings."

"That means, if there's no Orchid Village, then there likely isn't any construction office, and Winston's alibi would fall apart. Anything else?"

"Nope, that's it."

"Good stuff, Nina. I owe you!"

She laughed. "I'll add you to the list!"

The lieutenant hadn't said anything while Nina recounted the story, but when she was done, he smiled at her. "Good work, Detective."

"Thank you, sir."

Patton turned to Jason. "Any suggestion on further tearing at this guy's alibi?"

"Yes, sir. Will you get a subpoena for Marcus Winston's phone records?"

"Okay, on what grounds?"

"If there is no Orchid Village under development in Austin, we need them to verify his alibi."

"I'll take care of it."

Jason turned and went back to his desk. He sat down, opened the file on Marcus Winston, found the owner's phone number, and dialed.

"This is Marcus. I'm unable to take your call right now, so wait for the beep, and leave a message. Thank you."

"Mr. Winston, this is Detective Jason Strong with SAPD. I have a few more questions for you. Please call me here at the station, I would appreciate it." Jason left his number and hung up.

He scanned the file, and found the number for Norma Waters. She picked up on the second ring.

"Hello?"

Again, Jason noticed the lack of a business-like answer. "Ms. Waters, this Detective Jason Strong with SAPD."

There was a pause.

"Yes, Detective. How can I help you?"

"Is Mr. Winston in?"

"Well, no. I haven't heard from him today."

"Ms. Waters, I noticed I don't have the address for the construction office in Austin. Could you give it to me?"

Again a pause, longer this time.

"Well Detective, there isn't an office of the typical sort. I run everything for Marcus out of my home."

Jason wasn't tipping his hand. "Oh, I see. Okay, how about the address of the new Orchid Village complex."

"Sure. It's…" The phone went dead.

Jason called back. Busy.

He tried three more times, getting a busy signal each time. The phone was either off the hook, or she was trying to reach Winston.

****

A while later, the fax machine came to life. Vanessa went over and started pulling pages off one at a time. Ten minutes later, she came back with a thick pile of paper.

"Lieutenant got the warrant. I hate going through phone records. It takes forever, and this guy talks a lot."

Jason gave her a half-smile, and she sensed his mood. "What's with you? You seem a little down."

"Penny was hit by a car yesterday."

"Oh, no! Is she okay?"

"She had surgery last night and the vet said she'll be okay. Sandy blamed herself and was pretty torn up though."

"What happened?"

"Penny followed Sandy out to the mailbox, wandered into the street, and before Sandy knew what happened, she got hit."

"Scary."

Jason nodded. "All I could think was what if it was our child?"

Vanessa's face softened. "You can't think like that, Jason. I know there's a temptation to ask the what-ifs, but life is full of them."

He knew she was right. "Of course. Thanks."

She smiled at him and changed the subject.

"Now, let's divide these phone records up. I'm not doing all the work!"

He laughed. "Okay, okay. Give me the half you don't want."

****

They pored over the phone records all day, only stopping to grab lunch. During a mid-afternoon break, Jason called Sandy and arranged to meet her at the vet by four.

At three-thirty, he pushed his chair back. "That's it! Enough staring at tiny print for one day."

"Are you going to meet Sandy?"

"Yeah, and I imagine once we take Penny home, I'll probably stay there and call it a day."

"That's fine. I'm gonna put a little more time in before going home." She looked down at her notes. "So far we've confirmed Winston was out of town on each of the days we've looked at."

"Yeah. Or maybe just his phone was out of town."

"You think the girlfriend in Austin might have had it for an alibi?"

"Don't know, but until we physically put him in Austin, he's still a prime suspect. He has the best motive, money."

"True enough."

"See you tomorrow."

Chapter 15

Sandy was waiting for him when he got to the vet's office. She got out and hugged him. "I hope she's not in too much pain."

He touched her face. I'm sure the vet has taken good care of her, and she'll just be glad to go home."

They walked into the office and Sandy spoke to the receptionist. "We're here to pick up Penny Strong."

Jason thought it was odd that the vet used their last name, but after all, she was a member of the family.

"Great. I'll let Dr. Simpson know."

She got up, disappeared into the back, and a few minutes later, the vet came through the double doors with Penny.

Her big white tail wagged as soon as she saw Jason, but as if she instinctively knew, she hobbled right over to his wife.

Licking Sandy's outstretched hand, Penny seemed to be telling her everything was okay.

Sandy ruffled her white coat and leaned over to exam the cast. It ran from near the dog's hip, all the way down her leg, and over her foot. Dr. Simpson handed the leash to Jason.

"Here she is. She's not good as new, but I think she'll be fine. She had a dislocated fracture to the tibia, so we had to surgically reset it, and she'll be wearing the cast for several weeks."

Jason shook the doc's hand. "Thanks very much. I imagine she won't be moving around much."

"Nope. You can let her out to go to the bathroom, but then she needs to come right back inside. My assistant will make a follow-up appointment with you."

When the vet had gone, and they'd made the appointment, they headed to the car. Jason realized Sandy had still not said a thing, nor left the dog's side. As he loaded Penny into his car, he asked her if she was okay.

Sandy smiled. "I am now. I'm just glad to have our baby back."

He kissed her forehead. "Me, too."

******

He sat in his vehicle watching the front door of his last target's home. The mission would be done after tomorrow night. Finally, he would be able to focus on other things. His quarry this time went to bed earlier than any of his targets so far. The apartment was dark and quiet by nine o'clock each night.

Parked at the end of the cul-de-sac, he saw lights turn down the road, and he was ready. Lying down on his seat, he waited for the SAPD patrol car to drive by, a searchlight scanning the area.

The patrols were almost hourly now, and he'd be glad when he didn't have to dodge them any longer.

Of course, he knew he had created his own problem. Murder never stayed a secret.

He sat back up as the patrol car left him in the darkness. Tomorrow would be the first time he'd target two people in the same night, but they were both in the same apartment, and he was confident in his plan.

He would have to be quiet. No mistakes.

****

When he arrived the next morning, Jason found Vanessa already working on the phone records. The door to the lieutenant's office swung open just as Jason sat down.

Captain Garcia came out, nodded at the two detectives, and continued to the elevator. The captain wasn't on the third floor very often, and when the lieutenant came out to get coffee, Jason let his curiosity get the better of him.

"Captain stop by to rattle your cage?"

The lieutenant smiled. "Nope. Actually, I asked him to come by."

Jason waited for more information while the lieutenant filled his coffee cup and walked back in his office. He closed the door behind him without further comment.

Vanessa chuckled. "Guess that's all you're gonna get."

"Guess so."

****

Willie knocked on the door and waited.

"Who is it?"

"It's Willie."

The door swung open and Ruby stepped out, giving him a subdued hug. "Hi, Willie. Grace is almost ready."

He followed her into the apartment to wait. Ruby wore a long black dress, black shoes, and, in typical Ruby flash, a wide-brimmed black hat. Willie was all in black himself, except for the white shirt beneath his jacket. It was too warm for a tie.

It was the third time in as many weeks they had been dressed in these clothes, and the funerals weren't getting any easier. Today, they buried Tabby: the worrier who tried to keep them all safe, but in the end, couldn't keep herself from harm.

Grace came out of her bedroom, dressed much like Ruby, but without the hat. The strain of the last few weeks showed on her face. Like everyone, they wanted the maniac stopped, but they also wanted to know who he was.

And they needed to be able to sleep without jumping at every noise.

Willie bowed to his friends. "You ladies both look very nice."

Grace touched his face. "Thank you, Willie. You're very sweet."

The women gathered their purses as Willie opened the door for them. It was time to say goodbye to their friend.

****

Vanessa had just gotten back to the station with some lunch. They were still going over the phone records, making sure they hadn't missed something. Jason took a bite of his hamburger and set it down. Something was bothering him.

They'd gone through almost every call on the day of each killing. Nothing out of the ordinary. Regular business calls, but nothing absolute, putting Winston in Austin. Nobody to call and ask 'Did you see him?'

"This is getting us nowhere."

Vanessa looked up from her salad. "Okay, so what then?"

"We need to examine the days before and after each killing."

"That's hundreds of calls!"

Jason grinned at her. "You got something you'd rather be doing?"

"Yes! In fact, probably a dozen things."

Jason shrugged. "Me, too. Guess that's why they pay us the big money."

"Strong, they may be paying *you* 'big money,' but definitely not me!"

He laughed and went back to the phone records, this time focusing on the day before each killing.

****

It was nearly six in the evening when Jason looked at his watch. He called Sandy to let her know he would be late. They'd found something important.

Jason looked over at Vanessa, who was running a computer search on a phone number. The number she was checking was called multiple times the day before each killing.

Even more suspicious, Vanessa matched the same number to a single call on the day *after* each murder. It was always a call *to* Marcus Winston's phone.

The computer search finished.

"Got it! Oh, crap!"

Jason drummed his fingers on his desk. "Mind sharing?"

Vanessa jumped up and headed for the elevator. "Jose Jimenez."

Jason was right behind her.

****

Willie made sure Ruby and Grace were safely in the apartment before turning to leave. Ruby grabbed his hand. "Stay for dinner?"

He smiled at her. "No, I'm tired. Thanks anyway."

He kissed Ruby on the cheek and went to the door. "Lock this behind me. I'll talk to you tomorrow."

Grace followed him to the door and touched his arm. "We'll be fine. Sleep tight."

He left, and she locked the door. When she turned around, Ruby was watching her. "Nobody can sleep these days."

Grace nodded. "I know."

Chapter 16

The two detectives finally arrived at Jose Jimenez's small home around seven. Unfortunately, the evening rush hour had been in full swing when they left the station. The name 'rush hour' was definitely a misnomer. Jason thought 'Standing still hour' was a better description.

Jose lived on a quiet street in Harlandale, a working-class suburb in South San Antonio, nearly forty-five minutes from Orchid Village. The house was adobe red with brown shingles, and as you would expect from a gardener, the yard and flowers were beautiful. An Orchid Village truck sat in the driveway and Jason parked behind it.

"Looks like we caught him at home. Let's go see what his reason is for all those calls to Mr. Winston. I doubt they were gardening questions."

The two detectives came up the manicured front walk and pushed the doorbell. A middle-aged Hispanic woman answered the door. She wore a yellow housedress, covered with a red-checkered apron. The apron sported a large amount of baking flour.

"Hola!"

"Hola," Jason answered, and then gestured toward Vanessa. "Este Detective Layne y Detective Strong. Habla Inglés?"

The woman's face clouded over. "Un momento, por favor."

The door closed and Jason looked at Vanessa.

"Is your Spanish any better than mine?"

"You were speaking Spanish?"

He rolled his eyes just as the door re-opened to reveal a young girl, Jason guessed her to be six or seven, standing in front of the woman.

"Hello. My mother doesn't speak English."

Vanessa stepped forward. "What's your name?"

"Maritsa."

"Well Maritsa, my name is Detective Layne and that's Detective Strong. Is your father here?"

"No, not right now."

John C. Dalglish

"Do you know where he is?"

The little girl turned to her mother and repeated the question in Spanish. There was a rapid-fire exchange between the two before Maritsa turned back to the detectives.

"She said he goes bowling."

"Where does he bowl?"

Maritsa asked her mother and turned back to Vanessa.

"Bandera Lanes in Leon Valley."

"How often does he bowl?"

Another turn, another exchange.

"Every Monday and Tuesday night."

Something started bubbling up from the back of Jason's brain.

Had all the killings been on Tuesday nights?

He wasn't sure, but he wanted to find out.

Vanessa continued asking questions as Jason looked around the mother, trying to see inside the home. On the wall hung a picture that stopped Jason cold.

The photo showed three men standing next to a split-rail fence, each holding a trophy, a banner for the National Mexican Rodeo Championships in the background.

Jason interrupted Vanessa. "Excuse me, Maritsa. Does your father compete in rodeos?"

She looked confused for a minute, then turned to her mother, and asked her.

The woman answered with several long sentences, the little girl nodded her head, and then shortened it for the detectives.

"Not anymore. He used to do it a lot when he and Mama lived in Mexico."

Jason turned and walked for the car. Vanessa said a quick goodbye and followed him. "Where are you going?"

"I saw a photo on the wall of three men at a rodeo, one of which looked like Jose. You remember what Doc Josie told us about the knots used to bind our victims?"

"Sure, they looked like calf…" Vanessa was moving fast now.

They jumped in their car and raced for Leon Valley.

****

Jose sat in his car, watching the lights in Ruby and Grace's apartment. He had never met them in person, but he knew their routine. Within the hour, the lights would be out, and he would be able to move soon afterward.

He'd not seen any sign of life after they turned off the lights, and he was counting on it meaning they were heavy sleepers.

Another patrol came down the cul-de-sac and Jose lay down, out of sight.

****

It was after well after eight when Jason and Vanessa arrived at Bandera Lanes. The parking lot was packed with cars and, after not finding a nearby spot, Jason was forced to park on the Huebner Rd. They walked across the lot and into the noisy building.

Jason spotted the main desk at the far end of the building.

"I'll go ask at the desk. Do you want to walk around and see if you can spot him?"

"Sure."

Jason waded through the crowd, resisting the urge to show his badge and clear the way, until he got up to the desk. A young man, probably twenty or twenty-one, finished with a customer and walked over to Jason. "Need some shoes?"

Jason smiled. "No, thanks. Are you the manager?"

The young man shook his head. He had to yell over the combination of falling pins and conversation. "You'll find him working behind the snack bar. His name is Tommy."

Jason said thanks and went in search of Tommy. He found him filling soda cups behind the grill counter. His shirt confirmed his name.

"Tommy, are you the manager?"

"Yeah, can I help you?"

This time Jason did take out his badge. "Detective Strong, SAPD."

Tommy turned to a girl next to him. "Take over. I'll be back in a minute."

He lifted the countertop gate and pointed at an office across the hallway. Jason followed him.

Once inside with the door shut, it was much quieter. Jason figured Tommy used this office as his escape. The manager appeared to be in his late forties with a full head of gray hair pulled into a ponytail. His eyes showed a man tired beyond his years.

"What can I do for you, Detective?"

"I'm looking for a man; his name is Jose Jimenez. Do you know him?"

Tommy looked at the picture Jason held out for him.

"Sure, bowls every Tuesday night."

"Is he here tonight?"

"He was, but I doubt he still is. He bowls in the early-bird league, which starts at five-thirty. They're usually done by seven."

"Is he in the same league on Monday nights?"

"I don't think so," he smiled. "Monday night is ladies night."

"So there's no league he could bowl in on Monday nights?"

"Not unless he wears a dress."

Jason needed to find Vanessa. "Thanks a lot, Tommy."

Jason opened the door and let himself out. He was going to leave it open, but Tommy called after him. "Do me a favor and shut the door."

Jason pulled it closed as the manager reached for a cigarette.

****

Jason searched the crowd for fifteen minutes before he decided it might be better to wait out front for Vanessa. When he reached the door, he saw her standing there, waiting for him. "Did you see him?"

She shook her head and dropped in step with Jason as they headed back to the street, and their car.

"Nope. I guess he isn't bowling after all."

"Not anymore."

"I'm sorry?"

Tied to Murder

"I spoke with the manager. He said Jose bowls in an early-bird league and finishes about seven."

"Monday and Tuesday?"

"Nope, Monday is ladies night."

They arrived at the car and got in. Vanessa picked up the file on the seat, apparently thinking the same thing as Jason. After a few moments, she looked at him.

"All the killings occurred on Tuesday nights."

Jason fired up the car and Vanessa put the light on the roof. It was nearly ten.

Chapter 17

Jose moved as quickly and quietly as he could. The women had already been asleep over an hour and he wanted this over. Slipping his key into the lock, he slowly turned it until he felt the lock release.

After checking to make sure he wasn't seen, he cracked the door and stepped inside. Using the system that had been successful up to now, he stood in the entranceway, listening for the sounds of sleeping. A nightlight in the hallway cast enough glow for Jose to see where he was going.

He could hear steady breathing from the first room, but the door of the bedroom at the far end of the hall was closed. He decided to enter the far bedroom first.

Creeping down the hall, thankful for carpeted floors, he passed the first room and made it to the door of the second. Twisting the knob very slowly, the door opened a crack.

Previously, he'd been able to jump the victim and surprise them before they could put up a struggle, but he didn't have that luxury this time. He didn't want to wake the woman in the first bedroom.

Once inside the room, he shut the door, and let his eyes adjust to the darkness. The one he knew as Grace lay on her side, facing away from him. He moved toward the bed.

****

Vanessa called police dispatch while Jason navigated the dark streets. They were on the 1610 loop, heading for Orchid Village on the north side of town.

"This is Detective Vanessa Layne, who is this?"

Jason couldn't hear the answer.

"Okay Officer Briggs, I need you to call the patrols in the area of Orchid Village, and give them the following information."

Jason focused on driving as Vanessa gave the officer the description and plate number for Jose Jimenez's vehicle.

"I need you to pass the information on to them and have the patrols search the complex for the vehicle. They're to report immediately if they discover it. Give them my number and have them call me directly."

Vanessa waited for a response before hanging up, then turned to Jason. "He must have stalked the victims on Monday night, and then attacked them on Tuesday night or early Wednesday morning."

Jason jammed the brakes, waiting for a car to clear the intersection, before stepping back on the gas.

"Yeah. Clearly, his wife would not be able to keep tabs on him because of the language barrier. She couldn't just call the bowling alley and ask for him."

Vanessa's phone rang. "This is Layne."

Jason still couldn't hear the other end of the conversation, but Vanessa's reaction told him they'd found the vehicle.

"Which cul-de-sac, Officer?"

Vanessa looked at Jason. "Butterfly Lane."

Jason recognized it immediately. "That's Ruby and Grace's street! Tell him to park behind the vehicle, and call in backup, including ambulances."

Vanessa relayed the message while Jason looked at the time. Nearly ten-thirty, but they were less than two minutes away. When Vanessa hung up, Jason had an idea.

"You have the number for Ruby and Grace in the file?"

"Sure. You want me to call them?"

"Yes."

Vanessa found the number, dialing as the complex came into view.

****

Jose had just finished tying Grace up when the phone started ringing. He froze.

Looking back through a crack in the door, he saw the one called Ruby come out of her room. She was walking away from him as she went to answer the phone. He jumped up, but she got to it before he got to her.

"Hello?"

There was a pause as Jose closed the distance between them.

"Fine, Detective Layne…"

Jose hit her like a linebacker, knocking the phone to the floor, and pinning Ruby against the wall. Her head hit a shelf and she went limp.

He didn't know if she was dead or just unconscious, but he had no time to check.

Leaving Ruby on the floor, he hung up the phone, and pulled the garbage bags he'd brought with him from his pocket. He rushed down the hallway to finish off Grace.

****

Vanessa's face grew pale as the phone went dead. "He's inside!"

Jason sped down Butterfly Street. He could see the officer parked behind Jose's vehicle. They came to a stop, jumped out with guns drawn, and raced for the apartment.

****

Jose burst back into Grace's room to find her lying on the floor, next to the bed. She had rolled off, trying to get free. Her eyes flew wide open when she saw him come back in.

He grabbed her, dragged her back onto the bed, and slid the garbage bag down over her head. Pulling a large piece of tape from the roll, he looped it around her neck and started to pull it tight.

Suddenly, pain exploded in his head, and everything went dark.

****

Jason and Vanessa burst through the front door. "Ruby! Grace!"

"Back here!"

They didn't know where Jimenez was and had to move cautiously. Jason called out. "Where's Jimenez?"

"Gone."

Jason looked at Vanessa and pointed to himself, then the bedroom. Then he pointed back at his partner and toward living room. Vanessa nodded and moved to check the front of the apartment.

Jason moved down the hall and pushed open the bedroom door.

Ruby lay collapsed against the end of the bed, unconscious. Next to her hand lay a large, glass paperweight, the size of a softball. Blood covered one side of it.

He checked her for a pulse.

She's still alive.

Jason moved to Grace. She still had the bag over her head, but the tape hung loosely. When Jason removed the bag, Grace blinked several times before she saw her sister laying there. "Ruby! Ruby!"

Jason could see Grace was, for the most part, okay, and he needed to get to Vanessa. He untied Grace. "Stay put, shut the door."

Coming out of the bedroom, down the hall, and into the living room, he caught sight of Vanessa going out the patio door.

"Vanessa! You see him?"

"No, but I know he came this way. There's blood on the doorframe."

Jason ran toward the front door. "I'll go around from the parking lot, you follow him."

Darkness made for poor visibility, and Jason didn't know which way to go first.

****

Jose spotted the patrol car behind his vehicle as soon as he rounded the corner of the building. Ducking back out of sight, he touched his head. Blood covered his fingers.

He doubled back, heading for the rear of the complex, when he heard footsteps coming toward him.

Grabbing a rock, he pinned himself to the side of the building.

****

Jason stood trying to figure out which direction to go. A yell from the far end of the building alerted him to a struggle. He ran toward the sound, coming upon Vanessa on the ground, holding her head.

Jose reached for Vanessa's gun but Jason already had his out. "Jose! Don't do it!"

The gardener slowly stood up, leaving the gun on the ground. The officer stationed in the parking lot showed up and cuffed Jose, while Jason covered him.

Jason moved to Vanessa, who was just standing up. "You okay?"

"I think so. He was waiting for me when I came around the corner. I think he hit me with a rock."

Jason could see blood trickling down the back of her neck.

"You need to go to the hospital."

"No, I'm okay."

"Whatever. You're going."

She signified her agreement by sitting back down. An ambulance tech came up and started working on Vanessa. Jason went to check on Ruby and Grace.

Sprinting up the stairs, he found them being tended to by a different ambulance crew.

"How are we doing, ladies?"

Ruby looked up at him. "Did you catch him?"

Jason smiled. "We did. Were you the one who hit him?"

"Yes. The jerk flattened me from behind."

Jason laughed. Ruby seemed like she'd be just fine. Grace pointed at Ruby. "My sister saved my life."

Jason nodded. "Isn't having family around great?"

Grace nodded. "The best."

Chapter 18

Back at the station, Jason called Sandy to check on Penny. His wife was asleep. "It's late, what time is it?"

Jason looked at his watch. "Eleven-thirty."

"Is everything all right?"

"Yes. We just busted the Orchid Village killer, so I'll be a while longer. How's Penny?"

He could hear rustling, then a snuffling sound.

"She's good. I fell asleep on the couch and she stayed right next to me."

"Tell her I'm jealous."

He could feel, more than hear, his wife smile. "We miss you, too."

He hung up just as Vanessa came back from her visit to the hospital.

"How's your head?"

"Thirteen stitches, but I'll live."

He stood up. "They're putting Jose in interview room three. You want to go with me?"

"Sure, let's do this."

When they entered the room, Jose looked like a different man. The bravado of their previous meetings was gone. Vanessa leaned against the wall as Jason sat across from the gardener.

The first question was the most important to Jason. "Why Jose? What did these women do to deserve this?"

Jose looked at Vanessa, but refused to make eye contact with Jason.

"I had to do it."

"Why? Was it a compulsion?"

"No."

Jason wanted to feel sorry for the man—he was defeated and sad—but the memory of small Tabby was too strong. This man, whatever the reason, was a killer.

"How did you gain access to the units so easily?" Jose didn't respond, nor did he look away from Vanessa. Jason tried again. "Why are you and Marcus Winston such good phone buddies?"

At this, Jose looked at Jason.

"I want to make a deal."

Jason was caught off guard. "A deal? For what?"

149

Jimenez now stared at Jason, unflinching.

"If you want to know what this was all about, I'll tell you, but I want something in return."

"I can't authorize a deal on my own, but I'm willing to listen. What do you have to tell us?"

"Nothing until I get a guarantee."

"Okay, why don't you tell me what it is you want?"

Jose, who was back to avoiding Jason's eyes, stared at Vanessa.

"I want a green card for my wife, and a promise she won't be deported."

Jason knew the surprise on his face. He hadn't expected the request to be so selfless. The usual request by someone in Jose's position was to have the death penalty taken off the table, or leniency from the judge.

Jason thought of little Maritsa. "What about your daughter?"

"She was born here."

"Jose, I can't promise something like that."

"Then take me back to my cell, I'm done here."

Vanessa tapped Jason on the shoulder, nodding at him to go outside. Jason followed her and shut the door. "What's up?"

Vanessa looked over Jason's shoulder, through the one-way glass, at the gardener.

"Do you want me to call the lieutenant?"

"Yeah, see what he thinks about the request."

"What do you think he's got to offer us?"

"My guess is Marcus Winston."

She pulled out her phone while Jason went back in with Jose. He sat down opposite the gardener.

"Jose, if I'm going to get approval for a deal, I need some idea what information you've got."

The gardener stared at Jason, as though trying to decide how much he could trust the detective. Jason saw resolve come over Jose's face.

"Marcus Winston. He's the one you really want. I can give him to you."

Jason nodded. "Okay. I'll see what I can do."

When Jason left the room, Vanessa held out her phone.

"It's Patton."

Jason took the phone. "Lieutenant?"

"Yeah, Jason. Vanessa told me what he wants. That's outside my power to approve. What do you think he's got?"

"He claims he can give us Marcus Winston."

"Okay. Don't do anything until I call back. I'm going to call the District Attorney."

The lieutenant hung up, and Jason gave the phone back to Vanessa.

"He's calling the D.A."

****

Two hours later, Patton called back. Vanessa answered and listened. After a pause, she nodded at Jason. "Okay, I'll tell him."

She hung up. "The D.A. called someone he knows at the State Department. He can't *guarantee* the green card, but if the wife meets the requirements, he'll see her through the process."

Jason went into the interview room where Jose still sat. This time, he carried a small tape recorder.

****

Vanessa watched through the one-way glass as Jason listened to the story recounted by the gardener. The details were disturbing, and she found herself wanting to choke Marcus Winston.

When Jose was finally finished, Jason turned off the recorder, and sent him back to his cell. He'd been in the same chair for three hours, and he leaned back to stretch as Vanessa went into the room. "You okay?"

"Yeah, just exhausted. Can you believe that story?"

"Unfortunately, yes. I guess we're done for tonight?"

"Yes." Jason dragged himself up and out of the chair. "Tomorrow, Jose will help us catch Winston."

****

Jason managed just four hours sleep before he had to meet Vanessa back at the station. Jose was supposed to call Marcus Winston at a set time, and Jason had arranged for a phone trace to run while the conversation took place.

They brought Jose out of his cell into an interview room. Jason handed Jose's own cell phone back to him and watched as the gardener dialed the number.

"Marcus?"

A pause as Jose listened. "Yeah, it's done."

Jose looked up at Jason. Winston was throwing him a curve. Jason couldn't help him, and wasn't sure if the gardener had it in him to fool his boss. "How should I know why it's not on the news? I'm telling you it's done, and we're through!"

Jason could hear the owner scream into the phone.

"You're through when I say you're through! You got that?"

"We had a deal!" Jose screamed back at Winston.

"Well, the deal has changed. I got your wife into this country and I can see she gets thrown out!"

"I'm not killing anyone anymore. I can't do it."

"You'll do what I tell you. You know I can make the peeping charge come back. That'll get you thrown out, too."

Jason got the thumbs up. The trace had identified where Winston was. They already knew he would be in Austin, probably at Norma Waters's home. They had staked it out.

Jose kept him going. "You know that charge was bogus. You set me up."

"Cry me a river!"

Jason wanted to reach through the phone and choke Winston. He could hear everything Winston was yelling.

Jose kept at it. "I thought you said the number of units I freed up would take care of it. I opened up over a half-million dollars of unit sales. Surely, that's enough!"

"I'll decide when it's enough! There's still several units I want made available."

"But Marcus, I can't kill any more people!"

"You'll do what I tell you or the only one left in this country will be your daughter! Hey, wait, wait…what's going on here!"

The phone went dead and Vanessa came into the room.

"They've got him."

Jason took the phone back from Jose, who looked relieved to have it over. Not just the phone call, but everything.

"My wife and daughter are safe?"

"Yes. It's over."

Epilogue

It had been a week since the arrest of Jose Jimenez and Marcus Winston. Jason had been taking Penny for short walks, helping her regain her strength, and their pup's mood had returned to normal.

Sandy's pregnancy was beginning to really show, and they had another appointment today for an ultrasound. He and Sandy had decided to let the doctor tell them if they were having a boy or a girl.

After getting into the exam room, onto the bed, Sandy exposed her belly without being asked. The tech, the same one they had last time, squirted gel on her. After rolling the sensor around in silence for several minutes, she looked at Jason.

"Did we decide whether we wanted to know what we're having?"

Jason looked at Sandy one more time to make sure she hadn't changed her mind. She nodded.

He turned back to the tech. "We want to know."

"Well, have you chosen any girl names yet?"

Sandy beamed and Jason grabbed her hand. She was carrying 'Daddy's Little Girl' and he wanted to cry.

Nothing could be better than having another little lady like Sandy in his life.

****

After the appointment, Jason went in to the station to do some paperwork relating to the arrests of Jose Jimenez and Marcus Winston. Vanessa was there and she didn't give him a chance to get to his desk.

"Well?"

"Girl."

"I knew it! That's awesome."

He laughed. "Who's in with Patton?"

"Lieutenant Banks."

Jason sat down. "Oh. Again?"

"She marched in there a few minutes ago."

Jason shook his head. "I wonder what John did to get under her skin?"

"I don't know, but *I'm* not going to ask her."

"That makes two of us."

Just then, the door to Patton's office opened, and Lieutenant Banks made her exit. Jason and Vanessa kept their heads down as she flew by.

Getting off the elevator as Lieutenant Banks got on was Nina Jefferson. Nina came up to the Jason's desk as John Patton came out of his office. He smiled at Nina. "Jason, Vanessa. Welcome the newest member of Homicide."

Nina was beaming. She'd been a homicide detective in Austin, but had to give it up in order to move to SAPD.

Jason stood up and gave her a hug. "Congratulations!"

"Thanks, Jason."

Vanessa looked at the lieutenant. "Is this why Lieutenant Banks was so red faced?"

John Patton smiled, looking toward the elevator. "Yeah. I went to the captain and asked to have her moved over. Sarah was less than thrilled to lose her best detective."

Vanessa laughed. "That's an understatement! She looked fit to be tied!"

"She was. Maybe, I think I'll send her some flowers."

Jason shook his head. "I wouldn't do it, John. Stay clear, and hunker down!"

They laughed until they cried, all except the lieutenant.

He was just a bit nervous.

A NOTE FROM THE AUTHOR

It's hard to believe, but this is the fifth Jason Strong novel. I hope it has measured up to the previous four, and I'm sure you'll let me know.

So many have taken time to write and encourage me in this endeavor, and it is because of that encouragement that I am able to get motivated for the next book.

The characters continue to evolve, and even as I finish the editing on this book, the newest one is underway.

So, I hope you enjoyed getting caught up with Jason, Vanessa, and the rest. I look forward to seeing how they develop in each new book as it is written.

As always, thank you so much for taking the time to read our books. Contact me at my web page www.jcdalglish.webs.com or my email jdalglsih7@gmail.com. You can also visit Jason at his Facebook page: https://www.facebook.com/DetectiveJasonStrong

God Bless, John
I John 1:9

With Thanks to all who helped.

John C. Dalglish

Cover by Beverly Dalglish

**Editing by Samantha Gordon,
Invisible Ink Editing**

MORE BY JOHN C. DALGLISH

*THE DETECTIVE JASON STRONG
SERIES*

*"Where's My Son?"- #1
Bloodstain - #2
For My Brother - #3
Silent Justice - #4
Tied to Murder –#5
One of their Own – #6
Death Still – #7
Lethal Injection - #8
Cruel Deception - #9*

*THE CHASER CHRONICLES
SERIES*

*CROSSOVER– #1
JOURNEY- #2
DESTINY -#3*

Made in the USA
Middletown, DE
07 February 2023

24282119R00097